Dedicated to my dear friend Carol Clark
who taught me a lot about antiques
(and other stuff!)

MURDER ON AISLE 67

A Columbia Meadows Murder Mystery

ANNA M. LASCURAIN

Murder on Aisle 67 © 2016. (formerly titled Murder at Market Rate)

This book is a work of fiction. Names, characters, places, and incidence our prod- uct of the author's imagination or are used fictitiously. Any resemblance to actual events, locales, or persons, living or dead, is coincidental

CHAPTER 1

Somewhere lost off an exit of New Jersey Turnpike, hiding behind a world of green grass and horse farms, lay on underworld of curious goods and their strange purveyors. I am a member of that underworld, a vendor of the unique and unusual, most of which is acquired from my garage or basement.

Selling or reselling, I strive for an uneventful life. You get up, go to work, come home, and go to bed. The next day you do it all over again, the humble simplicity of a working girl. That was my life for, oh, a good ten years or so, and I was happy about it.

But that all changed the day I saw a pair of dead guy feet sticking out of a beat-up 1970s panel van at the Columbia Meadows Flea market.

It was seven a.m. on a brisk Saturday morning in March. The sun was up early, the weather, an unusually warm sixty-five degrees with a gentle wind. For the buyers, the hunt was on. Today Columbia Meadows Flea Market would change from rows of empty wooden tables to a bustling, energetic place, filled with customers eager to find that Rembrandt hidden behind a velvet Elvis painting. I watched as my fellow sellers unfolded tables, while others ran around trying to buy more stock. Everything from Victorian dolls to Belleek vases to vintage lava lamps poured out of some old truck or van.

I inhaled the fresh market air and caught a strong whiff of money; a perfect day to walk away with at least $500 in cash. I reserved my usual table with my selling partner, Karrie Langston. At her suggestion, we chose a corner table, intersecting two main aisles so that when customers entered the market, people traffic moved in two directions. We could nail them coming or going. We had lucky tables in Aisles L67 and L68. Table L69 was rented by Pack Rat Freddie, another regular vendor.

For the past three years, Freddie always took the table next to mine at Columbia Meadows. He'd been selling at the market for thirty years, and was a permanent fixture, not unlike the lamp posts or the Port-O-Potties. A chatty fellow, you couldn't miss the Pack Rat – shoe polish-black hair, an unfiltered cigarette dangling from his lip, and his loud voice screaming about the latest Yankee game. He drove a beat-up Chevy van with thick pile of dirty shag carpeting that never recovered from 1976. When Freddie arrived at market, he couldn't unload his van fast enough for the crowds. There was no organization to his table; he just dumped everything in a heap and allowed his customers paw through his stuff. He sold absolutely anything and everything, from sterling silver to naughty nudie photos from the 1920s, and old broken screwdrivers. Baseball might be a national pastime, but dumpster diving was his. Freddie tried to sell whatever he picked up from the street, no matter how useless or decrepit.

Me? Well, I'm a little pickier.

My name is Roxie Sanchez. I am a thirty-something single girl, a paralegal by day, with no taste for excitement unless it comes from a good garage sale or some spicy nachos. I'm about five foot six with long dark hair, and I'd like to say I'm a hundred-and-thirty pounds, but I think my skinnier days are behind me. I also have these big hips that are a Sanchez family trait. I know this because even our family Chihuahua, Polo, had the same butt curves. I prayed that as I aged, the spread of my hips wouldn't equate to the size of some Texas cattle ranch!

I supplement my salary as a paralegal, selling bits and pieces of childhood memories in the form of Tammy dolls and collectible Murano glass ashtrays on the weekends. If the prices is right, this stuff moves at Columbia Meadows faster than water through a strainer.

I looked over at the Pack Rat's table and noticed that it was empty. That was weird, because his van was there, and the back doors of the van were wide open. I walked over to the back of the van and saw a large pair of feet. The feet were wearing ripped-up construction boots with a hole in the right sole that had been covered up with duct tape all the way around to the toe.

I'd recognize those worn boots anywhere, and knew that they had to be attached to Freddie's feet. But with all the noise and potential buyers on the prowl, there was no way Freddie would have been catching forty winks at this time of the morning. That just wasn't like him. Too much money walking by to lose precious selling minutes.

Not a good sign. Something felt wrong; terribly, terribly wrong.

I knocked on the side of Pack Rat Freddie's van.

"Freddie! Oh Freddie! Wakey wakey time!" I yelled.

No response.

Then I made the biggest mistake of my life. I stepped inside his van, only to find old Pack Rat lying on his back atop his dirty shag carpeting with his string bean-lip smile, with a long cherry-red handled something sticking out of his chest. I couldn't scream, but I open my mouth and squeaked. Jumping out of the back of the van, I leaned against its rear quarter panel. My heart pounded inside of my chest as I tried to catch my breath.

I couldn't believe it. Pack Rat Freddie was dead. My stomach churned.

****

Taking out my cell phone, I dialed 9-1-1, babbling something about a dead guy in a van. I still couldn't breath, couldn't scream. I ran over to my flea market partner, Karrie. She would know what to do. I hoped.

She was carefully unloading a very lovely set of red vintage Fenton glasses with a matching beverage pitcher. I grabbed her arm, nearly knocking the pitcher out of her hands.

"What are you doing? Be careful!"

"Karrie! I just saw a body!"

"Really?" She yawned. "Was the body buying or selling?"

"I'm not kidding. It's Pack Rat Freddie! He's…he's lying dead in his van."

"Well my dear," Karrie said as she took the bubble wrap off one of the glasses, "I wouldn't get overly excited. You know, Freddie is notorious for having a few too many pops, many a night before the market opens. Maybe he got drunk and passed out."

"Oh sure, Karrie. People always pass out with things sticking out of their chests! Come with me."

Karrie must've finally paid attention to the panicked look on my face, because she actually put down what she was doing and followed me back over to Pack Rat Freddie's van. The police were already there, and now dealers and buyers drifted over to the crime scene. It was a macabre circus. Karrie casually moved in closer to get a better look. None of the police activity phased her at all, and she was poised and aloof about the whole incident. God, I wished I could be like her: total control, total calm, and yet a keen observer of human behavior.

She was my friend and fellow junk seller. Karrie had the gift of good genes, a tall and dignified lady of seventy who looked about fifty. Because of her height, she had no problem seeing over onlookers' heads. I watched her facial expression as the police carted poor Pack Rat Freddie's body away in one direction, while his van was towed in another. She viewed the scene, sighed, and then returned to our table.

I was still in shock. She shrugged her shoulders. "Oh my, the first wave of dealers is coming in. We really have to get back to business."

"I'm sick to my stomach."

"Sell something. You'll feel better."

"Don't you want to know what happened here?"

"No." She brushed a wisp of hair that had the audacity to move out of place, tilted her chin down, and looked at me over the top of large red-rimmed eyeglasses. "Freddie has been around for thirty years, and there were days when he seemed charming. He's actually a very nasty man. Nasty men meet nasty ends. I mean I certainly didn't wish him harm, but I didn't see anything and I have no intention of getting involved. Did you identify yourself on the phone?"

I nodded. "Yeah, I think so."

"Great, *you're* involved. Looks like you will have to talk to the police, and now I will have to sell my stuff and yours. Thanks a lot. Hmmf." Karrie rolled her eyes.

God, I hated when she did that. But I couldn't believe that she was all teed off about having to sell my goods. What if the police came knocking around and started asking questions. What was I supposed to do? Ignore them?

"Sorry to inconvenience you, Karrie. I didn't think that I would be looking at a dead body first thing in the morning. I wish I'd never looked in that van."

"So do I. Let's finish unloading."

Oh how I would like to go back to bed, I thought. *Will someone please take me off the crazy train?*

****

Columbia Meadows Flea Market was on the border of Howell and Farmingdale, New Jersey with one of its toes dipped farther into the map of Farmingdale. Because Farmingdale didn't have its own police force the way Howell did, New Jersey State Troopers took jurisdiction over the little town, which included Columbia Meadows. Uniforms were all over the place, talking to people and asking everyone if anyone had seen anything. Besides uniformed troopers, I saw some plain clothes detectives from Howell.

I kept a low profile, but I knew it would be a matter of time before someone found me. After all, I was the person who had placed the 9-1-1 call, and I was also the person with the misfortune of finding his body. As my rotten luck would have it, in the middle of all the craziness, a nice lady had come up to my table and was very interested in a beautiful Trifari hummingbird pin from the 1960s. I was just about to close the sale for a whopping ten dollars when a tall, good-looking police trooper interrupted my sale.

He was well over six feet with one of those high-and-tight military haircuts. He had epic arrogant blue eyes, the color of Arctic ice. He wore faded jeans with his badge attached at his hip and a windbreaker over a black T-shirt. My first impression, based on his size and the look of control in his eyes, was that he was an impatient man, and could be a very difficult man to handle…depending on who's doing the handling.

"Roxanna Sanchez? You placed the 9-1-1 call?"

"Yeah. I didn't see anything, if that's what you're going to ask."

"Let me ask you the questions, okay? My name is Detective Sergeant William Baines of the New Jersey State Police. Tell me what happened. You saw something or else you wouldn't have called."

"It's a simple story. Every weekend, oh, for the past three years or so, me and Karrie here have had the table next to Pack Rat Freddie. Today I went to see why he wasn't unloading things from his van, and there he was lying face up in his van with something sticking out of his chest. Now he's dead Freddie."

The Detective Sergeant never looked up. He just kept taking notes on a small pad. "You mean Mr. Selwyn Frederick Grant? Pack Rat Freddie is Selwyn Frederick Grant."

"That's his *real* name?" I looked over to Karrie. "Selwyn? Did you hear that? Selwyn." Karrie rolled her eyes and muttered something under her breath that sounded like "Who cares?" as she unpacked some Depression glass.

"I guess you call the guy Pack Rat Freddie because he buys and sells a lot of stuff."

"It was his nickname."

He looked down and kept writing. "He a hoarder?"

"Yeah, well, no, sort of. Look, if you are in this business, you're always a little bit of a hoarder. Pack Rat would buy and sell anything. I mean, he would buy and sell stuff most of us wouldn't touch. Like rusted tools, old tires, old lady underwear. I sell antiques, vintage jewelry, and vintage housewares. He handled more junky, uh, I mean more inexpensive items."

"When you looked in his van, did you see any inexpensive things, as you call them, inside the van?"

Now that was a real interesting question. I didn't spend a lot of time staring at poor dead Pack Rat Freddie, but I recalled that the van was completely empty but for his corpse. No way had Freddie showed up at Columbia Meadows without his goods. That just wouldn't happen.

"The van was empty. It was just him lying on his back, with the…the…the…that red thing sticking out of his chest." My heart started to rise in my throat. I felt sick…again.

Detective Baines seemed annoyed. "Calm down. What was this thing sticking out of his chest? What did you see?"

"I don't know! The thing that was sticking out of his chest. A knife, I guess."

"How do you know it was a knife?"

"I don't know. I just assume people stab other people with knives. I have to be honest, Detective Baines. All I saw was something with a red top sticking out of his chest. I was terrified. Didn't stay around."

"Is it a fair statement to say that you don't know what was sticking inside of Mr. Grant's chest, but you just assume it was knife."

"Uh-huh."

I watched as he looked away, distracted by something or someone else. "Listen. I have to talk to some other people here. Your telephone number is 732-555-4059? If I have any further questions, I'll reach out to you there. I want some more information about Freddie, that is, if you know anything else." Iceman looked over the top of his notebook. It didn't seem like I had a choice to make myself unavailable if he had more questions.

"Okay."

"Thanks."

He turned away. And his rear view melted into the crowd I noticed that he had some great walk away quality. I decided he needed a nickname, too, I would call him "Iceman." Maybe it was his warm and friendly demeanor that inspired me? Nah.

Apparently, I wasn't the only one who felt that he was attractive from behind. The lady trying to buy the hummingbird pin smiled. Her eyes followed the tall man in the nice fitting jeans. I guess she also appreciated a nice physique. Then she looked at me with a silly grin. What could I do but grin back, and sigh.

"Been kind of a long morning."

"I'll bet it has." She nodded. "Can you do five bucks on the pin?"

Aw, crap, I thought. *Well I only had a buck in it.* "Okay, ma'am. It's a deal."

She stuffed the pin in her purse and left. Karrie walked over. "You could have gotten twenty bucks for that pin on eBay and you let it go for five? Have you not learned anything from me? Squeeze money from these folks. S-q-u-e-e-z-e," she said as she made strangling motions with her hands. "Somebody says 'Five,' you say 'Eight.'"

"I guess I wasn't thinking. I'll do better the next time when I don't start my day with a dead guy."

"There's no next time for that pin, it's gone, gone, gone. Not trying to be unkind, but we are here to make money."

I unloaded the rest of my boxes from my SUV. Setting up for business, I made up,my mind to try and forget about the dead body I had just discovered.

****

Columbia Meadows was filled with characters. If Washington, D.C. was the think tank for the power elite, Columbia Meadows was the sinkhole for social dysfunction. The names and faces would have made Charles Dickens proud. You went by a first name or a nickname, but generally last names were *verboten* unless you were taking a personal check. If that was the case, you got first name, last name, driver's license and a quart of blood, preferably typed, along with a small child as a deposit. Except for taking an occasional personal check, everyone at Columbia Meadows wanted to remain anonymous.

The nicknames always fascinated me. Their monikers either identified them by their goods or by their looks. Doing this with Karrie for three years, I'd made many new and interesting "selling buddies" at Columbia Meadows. No one I wanted to invite home for dinner, but certainly they were cordial enough for the flea market world.

Leg and half Petey sold cheap toys from China, and swore that their paint had no lead content. Then there was Fishy McClure, an elderly man who sold vintage fishing lures and equipment. He had the hots for Karrie, although he looked like he could have been her father. Jamaican Janey or JJ, with her gorgeous caramel skin, sold lovely handmade things from her native Jamaica. She did some fortune-telling with cowrie shells on the side, ignoring the fact that the local township required a "psychic entertainer's license" in order to conduct such activity .

Bug Eye Betty, so called because of bulging eyes due to Graves' disease, dealt primary in the sale of dolls. Bug Eye and some of her Victorian dolls had the same kind of gaping, vacuous looking eyes.

I loved the Marias. Twin sisters from Mexico, the Marias switched over from house cleaning to cleaning out houses and selling their contents. There was Sarge, a former Army staff sergeant during the Gulf War, a quiet man who didn't talk unless he was selling. "No money, no talky" - that was Sarge's line. Lingerie Lottie was a bouncy, gum-chewing faux strawberry blond from Brooklyn, who had just ditched husband number three, and was dating an elderly retired judge. She sold collectibles and Victorian lingerie, which to my mind meant selling some stranger's hundred-year-old set of crotchless cotton bloomers.

And then there was my personal favorite, Red Hawk, who specialized in selling Native American goods and wares. We all just called him "Big Red." He was a Hopi from Chaco Canyon in New Mexico. Red became a New Jersey transplant, though he never told anyone why he left the reservation in Grants, New Mexico. Some thought he was on the lam, but he was always friendly and helpful. His personal life, just like the lives of Fishy, the Marias, JJ, Bug Eye, Sarge, Lottie, and to a large extent Karrie and me, was nobody's business. There was something sacred in Columbia Meadows's cloak of anonymity.

But now with Freddie's death, the cloak of anonymity had a real big tear in it. People were nervous. I was nervous.

A few of these folks lived, and some sadly died, in their vans and trucks. But it usually wasn't murder that did them in, it was old age and lack of healthcare. If a hardcore Columbia Meadows vendor lived into their seventies and eighties, it was nothing short of miraculous. Fishy, for example, was a walking wonder.

He was pushing eighty and still flirting with Karrie, having proudly announced that the Viagra was working just fine for him. Dressed in his Columbia Meadows finest, a broad brim Tilley covered with fishhooks and an old plaid shirt that probably could have walked to Columbia Meadows without him, Fishy came running over to me. He removed his Tilley and started tugging at the edges. He looked agitated, really agitated, and not because Karrie had turned him down for a date again.

"Roxie, the word's all over the place that you found Packy dead in his van. Bug Eye just told me. She heard it from the Marias."

"Yep."

"How did old Packy look?"

"Fish, he was lying there dead. How did you think he was going to look? I didn't stay around long enough to see if he was wearing a tuxedo."

"Are we going to do something for him?"

"Like what?"

"What's the arrangements?"

"I don't know. He just died an hour ago. If he was offed, the police may hang on to the body before they turn it over to the family. If he even had any."

"Who do you think did him?"

Fishy liked to talk, but the market was flooded with people. Not a good time to worry about Pack Rat's funeral arrangements.

"Listen, Fish, I have customers waiting. I'm on the verge of a minor nervous breakdown and Karrie is getting impatient."

And was she ever! She had a ton of lookers at some gorgeous Depression glass that she had just put out, but she was helping a woman with one of my items, a dented copper teakettle missing a finial.

"Yeah, Roxie, this place is crawling with people today. I better get back to my table." I watched as Fishy kept tugging at his hat. He wouldn't leave. I just looked at him.

"What?"

"Rox, are we in danger?"

"No, don't be silly. This is just, just a thing, a random bad act. I mean, it'll be fine."

"If you say so."

Suddenly there was a huge bear paw on my shoulder. It was Detective Baines. Iceman looked none too pleased.

"Ms. Sanchez, you and your friend here are going to have to move. We need this whole area. I spoke to Eddie, the owner. He says that he has a nice table for you somewhere else." He looked at a piece of paper in his hand. "Table 899."

I was not happy, and I thought Karrie would explode. Whenever she got angry, all you had to do was look at her ears. They turned bright red. When she heard we needed to be moved, it looked like someone had plastered two vine ripe tomatoes to the sides of her head.

"You can't do this to us!" I screeched. "We can't pack up and move now. We've just set up!"

"Too bad, so sad," he laughed. Before I could continue arguing with Iceman, he snapped his fingers and an army of his uniformed friends began picking up my stuff and moving it. I screamed at them but it was like talking to ghosts. They ignored my rant.

"That's fragile! What are you doing? You break it, you're paying for it, pal!"

I turned to look in Karrie's direction to see if she was right behind me, ready to take up the cause, and assist me in yelling at the police officers for moving our stuff. Iceman may have been irritating me, but it looked like he was sweet-talking Karrie. I listened as he explained that she and I would have to be moved to another table, because the area was now a crime scene. As Karrie batted her big blue eyes at him, her ears returned to a normal color again. He helped her pack, wrapping and placing fragile items in boxes. My stuff was dropkicked; hers was carefully tucked away by these big yet gentle hands.

I guess this means I'll have to turn seventy before I get any respect from Iceman.

I grabbed a box and followed the parade to table 899, our new selling station. Could things have gotten worse? It was the last table in a back corner of Columbia Meadows – Death Valley, Land of the Lost, dead man's land, point of no financial return. Nobody came back there, not even the feral cats who lived on the premises. If Pack Rat had died at table 899, it would have been weeks before anyone found the body. How were Karrie and I going to sell anything stationed in the boondocks of Columbia Meadows?

I looked at my cell phone for a time check. It was only eight-thirty a.m., but it felt like midnight was closing in.

CHAPTER 2

I live in a small apartment located on top of the Golden Lychee restaurant on Main Street in downtown Freehold. What more could a girl want? I was living the dream. An upscale loft apartment in Monmouth County with my own private entrance, a built-in washer and dryer, a private parking space coupled with the aroma of tantalizing Asian cuisine, excellent for a single person. That's how my place was advertised, and who could ask for more?

Okay, I could have asked for a more, a lot more, but it was all that I could afford.

My illegal apartment is a comfortable mouse hole, with a washer that leaks and a dryer that burns my underwear. My "parking space" is a block away from my apartment. The smell of oil, one step away from Texas crude, rises out of the Golden Lychee's kitchen and permeates my apartment. I tried to rid myself of the aroma by using air fresheners, but then the whole apartment smelled like lavender-scented egg foo young. The "private entrance" is right next to the Golden Lychee's garbage dumpster, and on a hot summer's night, you can inhale the scent of rotten bok choy. I guess I shouldn't complain much. I can walk down the street to the law firm where I work, and the place is affordable for someone in my salary range, which is one step above poverty level. I intend to hit the Powerball lottery or marry a multimillionaire and abandon my apartment over the Golden Lychee. However, for the time being, it's what I call home.

My little SUV was packed to the gills with boxes of goods, but not as many as I had started out with in the morning. That was a good sign. Hadn't had time to count the day's earnings yet, but I would do that when the car was unpacked. I opened the back door to my apartment and used an iron doorstop in the shape of a chicken to hold the door open while I ran up and down the stairs. After I had brought up the first box and was going down the stairs for the next one, Ying, the owner of the building and Golden Lychee, was at the bottom of the stairs. A short little man with a horseshoe of male pattern baldness, he was dressed in his cook's uniform.

"Rox-see, you need a hand?"

"No thanks, Ying. I have it under control."

"You work too hard for young girl."

"Have to keep the wolf away from the door."

"No, no," Ying said with a smile. "You need to let wolf in to pay bills for you. You pretty girl with long hair and nice shape, but you getting old."

"Gee Ying, isn't thirty the new twenty?"

"Yeah, but get too much girl into thirty, harder for girl to make nice baby." He demonstrated this by making concave motions over his chubby little belly.

I nearly gagged.

"How business today? Good?"

"Haven't counted out yet. Things were a little crazy today. You know Pack Rat Freddie?"

"Sure. Everyone in town know Freddie. He is my best customer. Eat at Golden Lychee four times one week."

"He's dead, Ying."

"Xiōng xìn." He shook his head. Ying seemed disturbed about Freddie's passing. "Xiōng xìn."

"You need to give me an English explanation, Ying. The last time I tried saying 'Hello' to your mother-in-law in Mandarin, I accidently called her a horse."

Chinese is a complex, wonderful language, but if you change the tone of your voice, a word can mean something completely different from the subject you thought you were talking about. A week ago, Ying's mother-in-law, Ming Ta, visited Freehold from New York City. Ying introduced me and I tried to say "Ni Hau, Ma-ah," which means "Hello, Mother." My tone was wrong and it came out "Hello Horse." Ying and the entire Wah family was amused, except for poor old Mrs. Ta, who yelled at me before she grabbed her cane and hobbled out of the room. I've decided to stick to Spanish. Much, much easier.

Ying laughed. "She is like horse, old nag. But what Xiōng xìn mean bad news, fateful news. Fateful news about death, no good thing. Freddie good man. Why someone kill him?"

"I don't know, Ying. I mean, look, he's just a harmless old man. He lived out of his van, probably slept in his van. And sold junk for a living. I sincerely doubt this is anything more than some random murder by a lowlife."

"Very sad. Let me know when and I and Mrs. Ying go to funeral. Oh, by the way, you have–" He rubbed his thumb and index finger together.

"Let me finish unloading, Ying. I'll have the rent check for you."

"Ah, never doubt you for one minute. Have a nice evening. Rox-see, I just prepare a nice broccoli cashew with rice. I save some for you."

"Thanks, Ying. When I finish up here, I'll come down." With that, Ying walked away and returned to the Golden Lychee. I knew his trip had a purpose. I was a few days late with the rent, and I guess Ying was worried. My recollection was that prior to my arrival, he had a bunch of students from Brookdale College stiff him for the rent. I usually paid on time, but I had to put a new engine in the old SUV, and as a result I was a little short on cash. I borrowed part of the rent money, and hopefully with today's sales I had enough for the entire amount.

****

By the time I'd removed the last box from my truck, I was way too tired to go down to the Golden Lychee for dinner. Giving Ying the rent check tonight or tomorrow morning would make little difference. I glanced over at the alarm clock on the little nightstand next to my bed. It was only eight-thirty p.m., but I was exhausted. I knew I had to get up and do this all over again tomorrow, and tomorrow was in a few hours.

The Sunday Columbia Meadows crowd was smaller, but I could still make some money selling my things. I had to pick Karrie up, and I knew she'd be ready at the crack of dawn. If I were late to her house by even minutes, she would be none too pleased. I forced myself to go to bed right away so I could be up at four-thirty a.m. to be at the flea market with Karrie by six a.m. or face her wrath.

I was never a really good sleeper, and at my age I never understood why. This night was particularly bad. I tossed and turned from one side of the bed to the other in a desperate attempt to relax. With every turn of my head, Pack Rat Freddie's face appeared in my mind's eye over and over again.

I hadn't known Freddie as long as Karrie had. I had been doing the flea market thing for only three years while Karrie and her ex-husband, Al, had been selling goods probably before I was born. They knew Freddie for at least two decades. Apparently old Freddie's looks hadn't changed very much over the years.

He had a full head of hair. It was as black as coal and always looked wet. He plastered it down, save a twisted curl that plopped in the middle of his forehead, using some stuff he called "pomade." One day I remember laughing to myself at Columbia Meadows because the sunlight reflecting off his black hair reminded me of sunlight reflecting off a newly tarred driveway. Nobody has hair that black and shiny, particularly after the age of fifty-five. Freddie was tall and thin, but he had this huge hang belly that traveled in front of him and resembled a barrel. Call it a beer or food gut, Freddie's protuberant stomach was legendary, not unlike his teeth. I recall he had about four on the bottom and five or six on top, none of which were neighbors. His smile, a barbarous jigsaw, and would have made excellent inspiration for carving Halloween pumpkins.

He usually wore faded jeans and a long-sleeved knock-off Ralph Lauren polo. The tired shirt had permanent food stains, disgusting reminders of Freddie's breakfast, lunch, and dinner menu for, oh, at least a decade. He smoked like a chimney, and on a good day when he had made a lot of money, he celebrated by keeping Wild Turkey Bourbon in a *Lost in Space* thermos from the 1960s TV show. He put a piece of masking tape across the front of the thermos, labeling its contents as "Space Coffee." I remembered all my encounters with Pack Rat Freddie, and one incident stood out with such clarity.

One time at Columbia Meadows, his broken down van had refused to start. I looked at the sky and noticed dark, dense clouds moving in pretty quickly. Karrie always had a good sense of the weather, especially when rain headed her way. She told me that her joints were the best weathermen. Wisely, she suggested that we start packing up immediately. We did. However, Pack Rat decided that the rain wasn't coming in and that the blackening clouds were meaningless. Karrie and I were ready to leave, while Pack Rat Freddie sat in his chair waiting for customers.

He had completely miscalculated, and the clouds were moving fast. Freddie had a desperate look on his face, which is why I think he hung around, hoping for last minute customers. Karrie left just as the downpour started. I ran to my car and started my engine.

I looked over at Freddie who was slowly placing things in his van. Many of the items he was selling that day were vintage photographs and paper goods, like old postcards and Jules. I got out of the car, ran over, and started grabbing things and throwing them in his van. He seemed surprised that I was helping him. He pointed to the open van.

"My back is out again. Just keep on tossing stuff in the van. Bought all this vintage paper and at an auction. If it gets ruined I'm going to be out about $700!" A loud thunderclap made both of us jump.

"Okay. You have any kind of order?"

"No!" he barked. "Just throw all of it into the van and I'll sort out the bodies when I get home. Get your tail inside that van, I'll hand you stuff. Now move!"

It was as though the thunder gods had taken a machete and split apart the raincloud right over Freddie's table. The water came down in buckets, yet somehow Freddie and I were able to load his truck with lightning speed. I couldn't wait to get out of the van, because the shag carpeting smell of decades of dirt, booze, and cigarettes. I was getting nauseous.

We had finally finished putting everything inside the van, and I raced over to jump back into my little SUV. I started up my engine and was ready to pull away when I turned and looked in my rearview mirror. I saw Freddie slamming his fist down on his dashboard. This could only mean one thing. His van wouldn't start.

Having grown up poor most of my life, I was very accustomed to fixing my own motor vehicles because I had no money for road service. I taught myself to do basic things like jumpstarting cars, change windshield wipers, and at one point, I was even changing my own oil.

When I finally got through college and got a job, road service for car breakdowns was the first thing on my list of presents to buy for myself. Most young women wanted new clothing, jewelry, gift cards for expensive restaurants, or vacations. I wanted AAA road service.

I ran back over to Freddie's van and knocked on the window. "Battery dead?"

"Yeah!" he yelled over a thunderclap as he pointed to the sky. "Angels must be bowling up there and it sounds like a strike."

"I have a set of cables. I can jump you." As I said the word *jump*, Freddie opened up his mouth and gave me a scary snaggle tooth smile. His face looked like a psychotic pumpkin, except this pumpkin could talk and had arms and legs attached to it.

"Jump me, eh?" he asked.

"Not that kind of *jump* Freddie. Do you want my help or not?"

"I was just funnin' with ya." He laughed. "Yeah, I think the battery finally went on this thing. After all, I bought it six years ago. Had to croak sometime."

It was pouring. Freddie hopped out of the van and grabbed one end of the cables while I grabbed the other. I opened up the hood of his van and started searching under dirt and rust for anything resembling battery terminals. Then I raised the hood of my truck and clamped the cables onto my terminals. We hooked them up to the terminals in the pouring rain, each of us quietly hoping that we wouldn't get electrocuted in the process. It would take at least twenty minutes for the van battery to charge. I asked Freddie if he wanted to sit in my car because there was no way I was sitting in his smelly old van. Much to my surprise, he came over.

"Freddie, I have some coffee that's still hot from this morning. Would you like some?"

"Yeah, it's kind of cold and nasty out. Little hot coffee may do me good."

"Here you go." I poured coffee from my thermos into a cup and handed it to him, watching as steam rose from the Styrofoam cup. I watched as Freddie took a sip of coffee, and his face twisted.

"Yuck! You put sugar in your coffee? Why ruin a good cup of coffee? That just ain't normal."

"If it's any consolation, it's artificial sweetener."

"Even worse." Then Freddie got quiet. "Thanks for helping, Roxie. Most people around here would have let me and my stuff get soaked in the rain."

"C'mon Freddie, we have been table neighbors for almost three years now at Columbia Meadows. How could I not help you? That just wouldn't be right."

"Interesting you say that. People around here don't often do things that are right. In fact, society often does things that are really wrong that harm innocent people in the process."

That was a deep statement coming from a guy like him. I had no idea what he actually meant, and Freddie looked at me in kind of a weird way. It was as though he wasn't used to the idea that people do random acts of kindness. He was almost pitiful to look at. I didn't get it. I had seen him at the market, and watched him in action. He really was a tough old curmudgeon. Wouldn't part with a nickel and would better deal another seller at the drop of a hat. But for one split second in time, Pack Rat looked like a lonely old man.

Twenty minutes passed in the blink of an eye. I poured Freddie another cup of coffee and watched him gulp it down. The rain started to let up. He opened the car door and ambled over to his van. He hopped in and turned the ignition key. I heard the ignition straining until the engine finally turned over. He got out, unhooked the cables from both our vehicles, slammed down the hood of his van and my truck, and then handed me the cables through my driver's window.

"Thanks. For the cables and the coffee."

"Any time."

Sometimes in life we get locked in a moment. The rainy day van jump start was my moment with an old man, now an unwilling member of the dearly departed.

I glanced at the alarm clock on my nightstand as I smashed the pillow on my face. It was eleven-thirty. I was rolling from side to side with my eyes closed, thinking about Pack Rat Freddie. What was wrong with me? Why couldn't I be dreaming of Brad Pitt?

Ludicrous, I thought. *Why am I thinking about this guy? I have family members I don't think twice about, so why am I thinking about some old burn-out from a flea market?*

I tossed and turned as I mummified my body in my bed sheets. Sleep evaded me, and I kept thinking about having to get up in a few hours. The "what ifs" in life will eat you alive. What if I had stayed in the van and tried to revive him? What if I had just found him a little sooner? And what if I can't get to sleep tonight? What if the murderer is still out there. This was so frustrating.

No matter what I thought, this man was dead. It was neither my fault nor my desire to have anything bad happen to old Packy.

Pleasant things, think of pleasant things, I thought, begging my brain to shut down.

Okay, what's pleasant? The view of Detective Baines from behind fitting every inch of his jeans. Karrie's fabulous almond cheesecake with a chocolate graham cracker crust. Ying's special broccoli with cashew nuts…

Wait. Oh no. Ying. His last words. "Why somebody kill him?" I never said that Freddie was murdered. All I said was that he was dead.

This night was never going to end.

CHAPTER 3

Sunday morning arrived faster than I would've liked. I guess I probably could have left everything in the SUV from the night before, but I didn't. After someone had broken into my truck a few months ago and stolen my stuff, I decided it was better to just unpack. So in the morning, I quickly repacked the SUV and picked up Karrie. She had less to sell today, so she would be traveling light.

"How did you do yesterday?" she asked. "In spite of the fact that they buried us in no-man's land, I still walked away four hundred bucks richer."

"Three hundred. I was really surprised. With all the madness, and considering we were off the beaten path, people still found us."

"We sell nice things, Roxie. I mean, just look around. You would not believe some of the garbage people will stick a price tag on and try to pawn off as antique."

"Are we back in the same place today?"

"I certainly hope not. I mean after all, how long can something be a crime scene?"

"Well, I'm not a police officer or anything, but I guess it depends on whether or not they're finished investigating."

"Oh this is ridiculous. Who cares about that old stink buzzard?"

"Karrie, c'mon. Have a little respect for the dead."

"That old wheeze? I am sure he'll be coming back from the dead just to resell the latest knickknacks he stole from another dealer."

"Stole? Freddie was a thief?"

"He most certainly was," she chirped. "My ex and I were still together when I'd found a genuine White Mountain Apache burden basket on another seller's table. I bought it for two dollars. Took a quick picture and sent it off to Blake and Faraday's Auction House in New York City. The last one had sold at Blake and Faraday's for $6,500. I knew what I had, I knew what it was worth. Was going to make lots of money on it, until that drunken no good bum fell into my table and smashed the basket to bits."

"Did he offer to pay you for it?"

"Are you kidding? Didn't even apologize. Didn't pay."

"But Karrie, that's not exactly stealing."

"Not offering reimbursement for something you destroyed is the same thing as stealing. He might just as well have run off with item."

"Look, he's gone now."

"Why, you know what they say, my dear. All rats meet fitting ends in the garbage dump of humanity."

"Karrie!"

When we arrived at Columbia Meadows, as usual the place was buzzing. Since our old tables were no longer a crime scene, we pulled up behind them and started unloading. Bug Eye Betty came running up to us.

"Oh my God! I can't believe you two are back in the same spot after Freddie died there."

I rolled my eyes. "Thanks for reminding us."

Bug Eye never ceased to amuse me. She wore a pair of men's coveralls with a bright floral Hawaiian shirt beneath it. Atop her head was a matching floral tam. She clutched a doll wearing the exact same outfit. She and the doll had the same eyes: two hardboiled eggs with pupils pointing in opposite directions like a chameleon. I couldn't decide which one made better horror movie material, the doll or Bug Eye. The doll was frightening. It was as though some witch doctor had thrown Bug Eye into a hot cauldron of boiling water and shrank her down to doll size. It was way too early in the morning to look at two pairs of Marty Feldman eyes.

"Can't believe we lost Freddie," she said, chewing on a bagel. "He skunked me on a few deals, but he was okay. Who do you think killed him? Heard he was stabbed, right? You saw the corpse first, right?"

I shrugged my shoulders. "I dunno. Ask Karrie." I looked at Karrie. "Any ideas, Karrie?"

"Fresh out and I don't care," she replied as she walked away.

"Wow, Karrie's a real ball of sympathy right there. Hey, how do you like my new line of dolls?" Betty asked, shoving her evil miniature twin in my face. "I call them Boppin' Betty dolls. Be a great buy for the kids at Christmas, don't you think?"

"Oh yeah. A real winner, that's for sure." *If you were selling to the Frankenstein family, I thought.*

"I think so, too. Who knows? Could be bigger than Barbie. Bought a whole lot of old doll heads and had to figure out what to do with them."

"Very creative, Betty. Hope you do real well with them."

"Thanks."

"Betty, I think you have a customer." I pointed to her table across the main aisle.

"Oh good. Time to sell dollies!" Betty ran over to her table, and Karrie and I watched as she shoved a Boppin' Betty doll into the face of a helpless old man who was examining some potholders.

Karrie walked over to me. "Stupid looking things! Looks like they were made by a witch doctor."

"Karrie, if it makes her happy..."

A wide smile came across her face. "Speaking of happy, I see you have a little friend, just coming for a visit." She raised a hand and waved at Detective Baines, who trotted not so happily down the main aisle of the flea market.

"Good morning, ladies. Mrs. Langston," he stated with a friendly smile, until he turned to me and nodded. "Sanchez."

"Hello." My voice could not have been flatter if a steamroller had run over it. "Any reason for you to grace us with your presence today? Plan on moving our table to another flea market?"

Karrie had already started batting her eyelashes. Butterfly kisses started flowing in his direction. I turned away, yet I felt his eyes burning through the back of my head. Something didn't feel right. This wasn't a social call.

"Is there any reason you're back, detective? Figure out who killed Freddie?"

He cocked his head. "Funny you should ask. Still working on poor Freddie." He picked up a boxed doll on my table. "A 1997 Holiday Barbie. How much?"

"Gee, you don't look like a man who plays with dolls. At least, ones that aren't blown up."

He looked at me like he had just bitten into a vinegar-infused lemon. "Nice, Sanchez. Very nice."

"Now detective," Karrie interjected, "my friend's a little tired, you know. We'll give you an excellent price on Barbie."

I felt like I was under a microscope. I had no idea where Karrie was coming from, and now a man, a very handsome man, who earlier treated me like the proverbial redheaded stepchild, wanted to make a purchase. Too weird for words. He looked for something, and I am sure it don't think wasn't 1997 Christmas Barbie.

He gave me the eyes, those incredible blue eyes. "How much?"

"A special price for you. A hundred bucks." I grinned knowing that he would be sufficiently shocked by the price.

He and Karrie jumped back at the same time. Then Karrie spoke up. "She's such a kidder. No, Detective. She means ten dollars, ten bucks."

"No, I didn't!"

He ignored me. "Sounds like a very fair price, Mrs. Langston." He turned to look at me. "My little girl is really going to like this. I am going to give it to her when I take her to the park next week."

I watched as he handed her a ten dollar bill. She carefully wrapped up the vintage new-in-box 1997 Gingerbread Christmas Barbie. "Thank you so much and have a wonderful day. You haven't heard anything about poor dear old Freddie, have you?"

He sighed. "No, ma'am. We are covering every lead, but we have only a few. Any ideas, Sanchez?"

"No, *Baines*, but if I get any Agatha Christie or Sherlock Holmes-like notions, I'll give you a holler." I slammed down an empty box just to make a point. He smiled back then strolled away with the Barbie doll under his arm.

Karrie was beside herself. "Seeing his little girl on the weekend? Makes sense. You see, I knew it. I smelled it. He's divorced."

"I'll bet he is. Probably because he's a cheater. I just got rid of one of those. Not interested in another."

I was introduced to a "nice" lawyer by one of the partners at the Freehold firm of Blackwood and Pynchard. He was a Texas lawyer who used our firm to "local" his presence in New Jersey for a trial he was starting in Monmouth County. If you are not a member of the New Jersey State bar you can't practice here, but you can get admitted through motion practice, providing a local firm vouches for you. William Clayton was a friend of partner Aloysius Blackwood, and Aloysius asked me to take Clayton around the Jersey shore in the off hours.

He was terribly handsome, really sexy, and one thing led to another. By the time his six-week stint was over, I was hooked on the tall muscular Texan. It was love, of sorts, at least for six weeks. When the trial was over, he swore a happily-ever-after with me, but told me he had to return to Houston to straighten some stuff out. Never quite told me what the "stuff" was. We planned on my moving there within six months. I was smitten and had packed up my SUV, ended my lease with Ying, and prepared to take a long drive out to Texas... until his wife called.

She asked if "Billy" had left an expensive cashmere sweater back in New Jersey. It was his favorite sweater, and she had bought it for his birthday.

I didn't mention that his sweater was in my bedroom, where he had conveniently forgotten it, after a long night of riveting sex. With every intention of delivering it to him in Houston, I kept the sweater in a safe place. But Mrs. Clayton was an innocent person who probably didn't know her husband was a cheating creep, so I put my shock and anger to the side. I told her that I believed I saw it around my office where he had left it after a meeting with my boss. I offered to mail it back to her after I had taken it to the dry cleaner to have a stain removed.

The detail that I forgot to mention was that *I* was the dry cleaner. I gave the three-hundred-plus dollar cashmere sweater a thorough washing in hot water and bleach, right before I tumbled it in my underwear-burning dryer on high heat. When she opened the package, I was sure Mrs. Clayton wondered why someone had mailed her husband a tie-dyed sweater that could have fit a Teacup Poodle.

I had no patience for cheaters. I figured the nasty good-looking cop was another Billy Clayton. Karrie disagreed.

"Why so negative? I think he likes you."

"I don't like him. Just let it go. Listen, I need to buy some stuff. Do you mind if I take a walk around?"

"Go right ahead, my dear. Looks like it is going to be a dull morning. Not a lot of buyers around."

"Thanks." I grabbed my purse and turned around just in time to see Fishy McClure stroll toward our table with a handful of wilted silk flowers.

"Karrie, here comes your payback for selling my doll to Detective Meany."

She frowned. "You are a dreadful child."

I waved at Fishy, then took the opportunity to bolt before I was locked into a conversation I didn't want to have. Moving through the crowds, I made my way over to Jamaican Janie's table. She was dressed in colorful garb, soft cotton skirts, and long dark braids with beads. Her face was a flawless caramel with fine, almost aquiline features. As I started pawing through a pile of costume jewelry, she gave me big portentous eyes.

"My girl, I was readin' de cowrie shells for you. I am worried. I saw be man chasin' you."

I sighed. "Janie, lots of men chase me. Bill collectors, mostly. How much for the costume stuff?"

"Twenty for de lot. One signature piece, a Marvella pin. Listen girl, I am worried about you. Freddie's spirit is with you. He wants your help." She paused. "In fact, he's standin' behind you."

"Janie, look. I feel sorry for the guy, but that is why God made police officers, to save lives and find killers. There's nothing I can do. I already told that detective everything I know. Here's twenty."

Janie took the money, but I sensed a seriousness in her that made me uncomfortable. "Roxie, be careful. I feel like you are in danger. Look sharp when you are alone." She reached into the pocket of her skirt and handed me a small drawstring bag. "Take dis. It is a little something for protection. Basil and bay leaf and a bottle of protection oil."

"Do I rub the oil on me?"

"No! Don't touch de oil. It's poisonous, pure belladonna extract. Just keep it in de bag and carry it with you wherever you go."

I swallowed. "Ok-k-kay. Thanks."

"No worries. Enjoy de jewelry. Now and make money." She added a note of caution, pointing a long leopard-striped fingernail at me. "But please Sistah, be careful."

I nodded. Before I could turn around, I felt that bear-claw-on-my-shoulder sensation again.

"Roxie, I caught the tail end of what Janie was saying. She's right."

Red Hawk Roberts stood behind me. Big Red was well over six feet and had long black hair that he covered with one of those Billy Jack hats. Dark eyes and a mischievous grin, I was attracted to Big Red, but I sensed the man had some kind of past that I wanted to know nothing about. Most of us Columbia Meadows peddlers lived in the area. People easily spoke of living in Brick Township, Howell, or Farmingdale. Where Big Red slept at night was a secret. Why he moved from the town of Grants, New Mexico, population 9,200, to sell Native American wares in a New Jersey town of 52,000, no one knew. He never spoke of a wife, children, relatives, or a past. And for what it was worth, it just didn't seem right to ask him about it either. Big Red was the mystery man of Columbia Meadows Flea Market. Every movement and word that came out of his mouth was steady and deliberate.

"You need to be careful. Freddie's spirit is restless." A strange breeze came out of nowhere, passed through the three of us, and then died out as quickly as it had come. "Here, take this." Big Red handed me what looked like a bunch of grass and dried flowers bound together by red cotton string.

"What is it?"

"Sweet grass and sage. Burn it to raise your prayers to heaven and cleanse your home of restless spirits."

"I know this is going to sound like a stupid question, but what about Freddie's spirit?"

Big Red tilted his head back and look skyward. "He'll be in touch." I watched as Big Red looked over his shoulder to his table on the midway. "Customers, ladies. Have to run. I think she wants to buy that dream catcher." He strode back to his table. I looked back at my own and saw Karrie frantically waving in my direction. People were all over our stuff.

Janie smiled. "Now back to your table and sell. Go make money!"

"You too!" I smiled back.

CHAPTER 4

Having recovered from my Columbia Meadows Sunday, it was back to the office bright and early on Monday at the law firm of Blackwood and Pynchard. It was my first job after college graduation. I had been there since 1993, and it's pretty much a nine-to-fiver. Other than periodic mercy raises that I wring out of Mr. Blackwood after throwing a hissy fit every two years, I earn a slightly-better-than-living wage with health insurance benefits that barely covers a sick housefly.

But I am a creature of habit who likes predictability. At the small firm of Blackwood and Pynchard, everything is predictable. It's almost like watching coffee drip.

Every Monday Aloysius "Old Rainey" or Blackwood saunters into the office at around 9:45 after a hard weekend of golf or sailing, depending on the weather. At sixty, faking the looks of a shriveled man of ninety, Big Al Blackwood was working on what he hoped would be wife number four: Eva Lee, a busty forty-something secretary he had just hired.

Al was the partner who generated almost all the firm's income, the rainmaker, and gave himself the moniker "Old Rainey." He was loud, demanding, and often talked about himself in the third person, sing-songing, "Old Rainey would like a coffee now," or "Old Rainey wants you to get in touch with that Mr. Wills and find out where his retainer money is." Despite his numerous eccentricities, Al Blackwood had a big heart. He was an excellent trial lawyer, when his mind was put to it. He rarely wrote a brief and believed that legal cases were won on the strength of oral argument rather than the written word. He only wheeled into court for important oral arguments or jury trials, but he was a tremendous force to be reckoned with inside the courtroom.

Not so much with his partner, Edward Auburn Pynchard, III who basically attached himself to Old Rainey's legal coattails. A short sinewy man with an impeccably groomed moustache, Edward Pynchard was my least favorite person at the firm. Wound tighter than a Tesla coil, he was condescending and often treated support staff like dirt. He was a quiet, underhanded bully, the kind of guy who liked to light fires between staff members, then watch from afar with enjoyment as the relationships burned. Pynchard fancied himself the firm's legal intellect and its best writer. To me, he was nothing more than an elitist wordsmith whose legal writing was as dry as old sawdust.

Rumor was that he wasn't always like this; he was up for partnership at a major Manhattan firm and was passed over twice. Pynchard's judicial nomination in New York went the way of the dinosaur because of a change of political parties. What can I say? We don't always get the things in life we want, right? But instead of moving on from his disappointment, he took it out on his employees, me being one of the abused. "Coldstone Pynchard" was nobody's pleasure to work with or for.

Big Al may saunter into the firm every day at quarter to ten, but Pynchard parades in every day at nine o'clock sharp, occasionally muttering a "Good morning" under his breath, if the mood strikes him. Despite his own delusions of adequacy, the firm's real intellect was someone entirely different and unpretentious.

Macoun Ferguson was a permanent associate at the firm. He was shorter than me with a shock of thick brown hair that he wore like Edward Kennedy. Cherry red suspenders held up his pants, which made the hems just short enough to show the world his mismatched socks. The fact that these suspenders supported Mac's pants over his large stomach was no less an architectural wonder, like the suspension cables supporting the Brooklyn Bridge. He had exactly two white shirts, which he switched off at the local cleaners each week. I know this is because I dropped the dirty one off each week and picked up the clean one every Thursday.

Pynchard may have had the degree from Yale University, but Ferguson was the firm's intellectual muscle. Even Old Rainey knew that when he needed a complex legal issue briefed, Mac Ferguson was the one he wanted. This was a thorn in the paw of the old Ivy League lion, because Pynchard could never accept that an unassuming, chubby chatterbox had one up on him in brain power. Ferguson created the legal arguments. Big Al and Pynchard presented them in court.

I adored Mac. He was always in at seven-thirty in the morning, puttering around, looking for his old high school girlfriend on the internet. Work and his elderly mother who lived with him was his family. Freddie's death intrigued Mac, but made him nervous at the same time. He hated violent endings even in movies.

The whole murder thing had worn me out this weekend. It would be good to be part of the regularity of the office: Big Al ordering his coffee, Pynchard brooding in his office, and Mac lecturing secretaries on the mating habits of fruit flies based on an article he read in National Geographic. If working at the firm was like watching drip coffee perk, then today I was happy to drink the first cup. I looked forward to a normal day.

But that was not what the universe had in store for me today.

I had barely taken my coat off when Pynchard waved me over. "In the conference room, NOW!" He turned on his heel, and I looked at two other support staff, Madge and Kathy, wondering if they would be cleaning out my office in a few hours.

"Well, I guess he doesn't know that I'm not blind or deaf." I walked over to my cubicle, grabbed a legal-size pad, and ran into the conference room.

Putting my hand on the doorknob, I took a deep breath. My guts were twitching. I mentally ran over the cases I had been working on to see if I had missed a date on something. Maybe I filed a motion with the exhibits out of order. Maybe I didn't jot the right number down on a telephone message. Whatever aroused Pynchard's ire had something to do with me, which meant this meeting was going to be a real dirt fest. I wondered who would lob the first stink bomb at the other.

When I opened the door, my heart sank. A laptop and a projection screen was set up. At the head of the table was Big Al, next to him was Pynchard, then two other gentlemen whom I didn't know. And finally in all his Darth Vader-type glory, sat Detective Baines. I suddenly knew what Custer felt like at the Battle of Little Big Horn. And these weren't friendly Indians.

Big Al spoke first. "Now Roxie, you have nothing to worry about. You aren't in any trouble."

"Okay."

"Do you know everyone in the room?"

I looked over at Baines. "Not everyone."

"This is Detective Baines from the State Police."

"Him I've met."

"The gentleman next to him is from the Monmouth County Prosecutor's Office, Homicide Unit, Assistant Prosecutor Wink. The gentleman next to him is the estate lawyer for Mr. Grant's estate, Mr. Queecy."

I looked at him. "His name is Mr. Queasy?"

The estate lawyer looked annoyed. "The proper pronunciation is capital Quee-Cee."

"What does this have to do with me?"

"You'll see. Roxie, can you darken the room for us?"

I flipped the light switch and sat down at the table. I had this sinking feeling in the pit of my stomach. And worst of all, whatever was wrong today had to do with poor dead Fred.

"What is this about?"

"As I explained, Roxie, you haven't done anything wrong. But I would like you to take a look at this DVD."

"Well, I'm really kind of busy."

Big Al ignored the remark. Detective Baines clicked the mouse attached to the laptop. At first, I saw a blank blue screen with a microphone. And then in all of his glory, Pack Rat Freddie waltzed onto the screen. I was shocked.

His appearance was different, very different, from the man I had known at the flea market. He was wearing an expensive silk tie, a wristwatch, an Armani suit, and actually looked well groomed. His hair was washed and combed, not greased down to his scalp. He smiled and must have put in a bridge because he had a full set of white teeth.

I could hardly believe that this was the same dirty, grimy guy I knew from Columbia Meadows. He tapped the microphone, then turned to whoever was filming the event and said, "Are we ready to go? Hey, Lou, make sure you zero in on the watch first…"

The videographer took a close-up of the Patek Philippe watch on his wrist. I couldn't believe it. I didn't think Freddie could even spell Patek Philippe.

"Okay, good. Today is April 1, 2017. My name is Frederick Selwyn Grant, and I am of sound mind and body. Of course, the body isn't quite what it used to be, and since ya never know when the Big Man in the sky is going to call you, I am, therefore, using this here video as my last will and testament. If you are watching this video, I am probably as dead as a doornail by now. Oh well. Too bad. Wait, hang on folks, I need a smoke."

Freddie then reached into his breast pocket, pulled out a crumpled pack of Marlboro cigarettes, lit up, and blew a smoke ring as he continued his monologue.

"I have chosen to do this by video," he said exhaling another nicotine cloud, "for a very simple reason. I want to be clear. Very, very clear. The people mentioned in this video meant something to me and are getting part of my estate. I also want it to be known that if you are not mentioned in this here video presentation, you don't get a slug nickel from me. This includes my two fat, useless sisters, Jule and Lorelei Grant. Oh wait, I think they been married a few times, they have different last names, each is on a third husband, I think. Those two hags burn through husbands the way I change my drawers. Every three weeks! Ha!.."

"Oh dear God," I said aloud.

"… No doubt before I am even planted somewhere, the gruesome twosome will come sucking around, looking for my money. Anyway you'll recognize 'em. Can't miss 'em. They look just like me, except they have better mustaches."

Everyone in the room chuckled except Pynchard.

"So I'm here to say, I bequeath my estate in several portions. I leave to my Masonic brothers $100,000 for the Liberty Tree Lodge Number 33. These funds are to be used to help kids walk because that's what us Shriners do. To my car mechanic Ed, you always gave me a break and helped keep that piece of crap van running for a life much longer than it deserved, so I'm giving you $50,000. You can put that addition you wanted on the house, this way you can take in your mother-in-law and father-in-law. To my lawyer Mr. Alfonse Queecy, now I know you always said it 'Quee-Cee,' but you'll always be 'queasy' to me. Ha! I am making you the executor of my estate. Take out whatever it is that executors take for distributing dead guy stuff. You've always been a little stiff, but I think you're a decent and honest man."

I had no idea what he was talking about, but I was completely unprepared for his last set of statements.

"And as for the remainder of the estate, I leave it to that cute little Puerto Rican chick that used to work next to me in the flea market, Roxie Sanchez. Roxie, you are a goodhearted slob just like me, and you deserve a break. I'll never forget how nice you were to me that one time when it was raining. Random kindness is rare. You are a good soul. I leave the remainder of my estate to Roxie Sanchez, which includes my home in Colts Neck, my van, my various and sundry collectibles, and everything else. Oh and in addition, you get my pride and joy, my boat, the *Bearded Lady*. I moored it at the Parsells Marina down in Point Pleasant, New Jersey. Spent many happy days clamming and crabbing with the *Lady*, and I'm sure you will enjoy it, too. Ah, yes. Breathe the sweet salt air, looking at Antares – that's all a man needs, to see Antares. Everyone should look at Antares in August."

He paused and looked very serious. "Everyone *must* see Antares. Oh, and by the way, I have changed my mind about leaving something to my sisters." He put the cigarette out in a nearby ash tray.

"Just to make a point clear, I leave to my sisters, Jule and Lorelei, the sum and substance of ten cents to be split between them in equal amounts. And this is more generous than you two witches probably deserve, but hey, I am a generous man. I'm not incompetent, not drunk – well, at least not today – and this is how I want it. And Alfonse, I know I never told you about this video, but I didn't want to. Surprise to everybody! And happy hunting! Oh, and a few more things. After Roxie plants me, I would like a Masonic prayer at my funeral, and a drunken bash afterward for all my friends at Columbia Meadows – Bug Eye, Lottie, Fishy, Red Hawk, Sarge, and anyone else." Freddie turned, stood up, and looked in the direction of the person filming his last will and testament. "I guess we're done here, right boss?" He gave a salute then whistled, "Too-da-loo! And just like the Pink Floyd song, see you on the Dark Side of the Moon!" At which point with cheerful aplomb, he turned his big old back to the camera. He dropped his suit pants. As he bent over, the video camera zoomed in on a pair of old man boxers shorts covered in kissy lips and pink flowers. Freddie's wild guffaws echoed in the background.

The screen, like my mind, went blank. Someone flipped the light switch. I looked at the faces seated around the conference table. Baines grinned. Queecy adjusted his glasses, dabbed the sweat beading on his forehead, and kept a poker face. Looking upward toward the ceiling, Mr. Wink tapped his lip with his index finger. It was as though he contemplated something unrelated to this murder, like wondering if he'd left a faucet running in the bathroom before he left for work this morning. A sullen Pynchard finger drummed on the conference table. Big Al broke the mood and started to speak.

"That was certainly colorful enough. Now I'm sure this makes no sense to you, but as you know this is a homicide. And Assistant Prosecutor Wink and Detective Baines have certain concerns, as does Mr. Queecy here. What's the matter, Roxie? You look like you have just seen a ghost."

"I'm in shock. What can I tell you? I know nothing about any of this. The only thing I know is that I found his body. I've told Detective Baines everything I know. I wasn't expecting to be in the will of some dead guy I barely knew." I looked at all the faces of the men seated at the conference table. It seemed to me that no one believed a word I said. I was terrified.

Big Al continued. "As I said before, you didn't do anything wrong. Well, at least no one here thinks you did. I know that you've been doing the flea market thing for a couple of years now. Tell me. Is there any reason a complete stranger would leave you the bulk of his estate?"

"I don't know. I'm really as surprised about this as you are. I mean, I only knew Freddie from the flea market. That's about it. I mean, you know, he was kind of a bum. I helped him out once when his van broke down, but that was a long time ago." I looked over at Mr. Queecy. "What am I supposed to do now?"

The elderly lawyer adjusted the wire-rimmed glasses balancing precariously on the tip of his nose. "It seems to me that we have to get a handle on what exactly is in Mr. Grant's estate. The estate must be probated. At this point, I am not even sure if the money he's talking about is still there or what kind of condition the Colts Neck house is in. I need to file letters testamentary with the Surrogate's Office. I was actually going to go out to the Point Pleasant Marina space to see what the *Bearded Lady* looks like – the boat I mean. Who knows if it survived Hurricane Sandy? If it's the boat I'm thinking about, it's a dilly."

"Dilly? What about his house, Mr. Queecy?"

"I'm sorry, Ms. Sanchez. I've never been to Mr. Grant's house. He would always come to my office. I have no idea what it's like. The address is 10 Old Manor Road, Colts Neck, right near the downtown Freehold border."

"Can I go there now and look around inside?" I thought there'd be no harm in having a peek. As of right now I was the owner of the property. Well, sort of an owner. I was surprised when Mr. Queecy jumped all over that one.

"No, no. That would be ill advised, Ms. Sanchez. Title doesn't pass to you until the estate is probated. There may be problems with the estate. It could be challenged by Jule Mustergrave and Lorelei Kranz, his sisters. And if the property were damaged in any way –well, I think you should stay away from Old Manor Road."

It was interesting the way everyone sort of stared at me. All the men in the room were looking at me like I had a third eye growing out of the middle of my forehead. On one hand I was being told that I wasn't in any kind of trouble, yet on the other hand I felt that there was some kind of an undercurrent here. The homicide prosecutor and my good old buddy Detective Iceman said nothing to me. I expected them to ask me a ton of questions, yet the room was oddly silent. Gnawing at me was this feeling that there was something I didn't know about this whole situation. And then an interesting suggestion arose from Mr. Queasy.

"You know, Ms. Sanchez, if you wish to completely renounce the Grant estate, no one would fault you for it."

"Why would I want to renounce the estate?"

"Oh, please, Ms. Sanchez, please don't think I'm trying to discourage you. But you know there are certain responsibilities that come with being an heir to an estate. This probate process often takes a long time. And sometimes the only people who make any money out of the estate are the attorneys. Nevertheless, you have my word that I am going to do everything I can to preserve this estate. Even in nice areas like Colts Neck, when people find out someone has passed on…well, I am sure you know the rest."

I didn't know what was ahead of me, but there was no way that I would permit myself to be pushed out of money. I mean, it's not like I had a family supporting me or anything like that. I have a sister, Angela, but she is a single mother with three little kids. My parents had passed away a long time ago. They were simple people and didn't have much of an estate. When they passed on, I barely had enough money to bury them with some meager insurance proceeds. I didn't know what I would find with Freddie's stuff, but I certainly wasn't going to renounce anything until I knew what I had. I figured if Freddie had two sisters fighting for access to his assets, my eccentric friend may be worth big bucks. Who knows? Maybe Freddie was richer than Bill Gates, but if I didn't explore what was in the estate, I would never know. Sometimes life throws you strange presents at you. Maybe this was a present for me.

"No. I understand the need for someone to look after a house. I think that I would just like to see this thing through, Mr. Queecy. I am not renouncing the estate at this time."

I watched as Mr. Queecy's mouth twisted uncomfortably. "Very well then," he said. "If that's the choice you've made I will be more than happy to work through the estate process with you. What is most important right now, Ms. Sanchez, is to have a full accounting of all the estate assets. That has to be done before any distributions can be made."

Big Al smiled and chirped up. "Roxie, our firm will be happy to help you with this estate matter at the family rate. I realize that this is a difficult time for you, but you've been working at this firm many years now. You are part of the Blackwood and Pynchard family whether you like it or not."

Oh yeah. *Family*. I was just feeling the love vibrations. It was easier for me not to make waves and try to do whatever was asked of me.

"Mr. Queecy, there's no way I can take a look at that Manor Road house?"

"I wouldn't advise that at this time, Ms. Sanchez."

That was all I needed to hear. Soon it would be summertime, and the days were already starting to get longer. It was the perfect opportunity to do a little snooping on my own.

And Manor Road was calling.

CHAPTER 5

I continued doing my day-to-day work at the firm, and at night as I lay in my bed, I saw visions of Freddie running through my head. I wish that they could've been visions of sugarplums, chocolate sundaes, naked athletic men, or even a crème brulee. But instead I kept thinking of Freddie and his Armani suit, some boat named the *Bearded Lady*, and a mystery house I now owned on Old Manor Road. I wanted to see it. The more I thought about it, the more I realized there was only one person to enlist in my exploration of the Old Manor Road house: Karrie.

And she couldn't wait to see where all this was going.

I left work a little early and picked Karrie up in my SUV at four o'clock. She stepped up into my car, complaining from the moment I popped the door locks to let her in.

"Do you think you could have bought a higher vehicle? For the love of Pete, I'm not a gazelle, and I just had a knee replaced."

"Come on, Karrie, stop whining and hop in."

When she sat down, she pulled a map out of her pocketbook. As she unfolded it, she started to tell me why she thought maps were better than a GPS. "People rely on all that computer stuff. But they forget the basics. Maps were around much longer than GPS. I would still rather look at a map than a computer screen. Anyway, the place that we're going is right on the border of Freehold and Colts Neck, although according to the map, Freddie's house is in Colts Neck."

Karrie and I drove down Main Street until it ended and turned into Route 537. The farther away we got from downtown Freehold, the more spacious the houses became. We made a left turn onto Old

Manor Road and started to see horse farm after horse farm. It was a little past four o'clock.

"I can't believe he lived in Colts Neck. I thought he lived in a trailer somewhere. Who would have thought Freddie even owned a house, let alone a house in Colts Neck?"

"What I don't understand, Roxie, is why he would leave anything to you."

"Thanks a lot! That makes me feel good."

"Now Sweetness, you know I adore you. It's nothing like that. I'm not jealous or anything, but sometimes you wonder what goes through people's minds in cases like Freddie's. When you watched the DVD of him at the lawyer's office, did he say anything strange in the video?"

"The whole thing was strange, but he said something about Antares in August. He has a boat at the Point Pleasant Marina called, I think, the *Bearded Lady*..."

"Oh how ridiculous. What a silly name for a boat!"

"He has the house and I guess there must be bank accounts somewhere, because he is leaving his fellow Masons a hundred grand, and he's leaving his garage mechanic like fifty grand. He says he's also leaving me all his collectibles. Oh great. A bunch of broken shovels. Why couldn't he leave me the hundred thousand?"

"I have a practical question. Are you responsible for burying him?"

"Yes, and throwing a repast afterward."

"Did he really moon..."

"Yes, don't remind me. I could've gone my whole life without seeing that."

"See, I told you he was a dreadful fellow, and now he's a *deadful* fellow."

I sighed and re-directed the conversation. "Since it's a homicide, I'm sure they're going to hold on to the body for a few more days."

"Then you'll have to stick that bum in the dirt afterward."

"Karrie!"

"Change of subject. How is that handsome detective doing with the whole homicide investigation?"

"I don't know. He was at the meeting and watched the last will and testament video along with the prosecutor."

As we drove down Old Manor Road, we passed horse farms continued to be mingled with luxury homes. I kept thinking to myself that it was hard to believe that Freddie could ever have lived a wealthy lifestyle. I was really surprised to see him in the video with an expensive suit, and some teeth in his mouth, particularly after he had admitted that he only changed his underwear every three weeks.

It was about four-thirty p.m. I watched as the spaces between farms grew wider and the numbers on these estates got lower and lower. Freddie's house was number ten. When we passed a horse farm whose address was 20 Old Manor Road, I began to get really excited. I think Karrie felt the same way. Freddie was in the business for almost thirty years. With any luck he would be hoarding some wonderful collectibles that I could sell at Columbia Meadows.

"Karrie, you see anything?"

"We must be getting close. But I'm sure he didn't live on one of these million-dollar farms."

"Hey, you never know."

Karrie was like a second mother to me. I spent holidays at her house, and I called her every day just to tell her how I was doing. We met at Columbia Meadows, and it was just one of those friendships that started off the right way. She was so knowledgeable about antiques and collectibles, and I learned so much from her. But she can be tough and no nonsense.

"Slow down, Roxie. I think we're getting close."

I suddenly found myself at the end of Old Manor Road with no house in sight. After passing horse farms and luxury mansions, there was no number ten. Karrie looked at her map.

"Are you sure you don't want me to turn on the GPS?"

"No!" she barked. "Maps were made long before those GPS things. Let's follow the map."

"Oka-a-ay."

"This road continues. We have to keep going."

"I don't get it. Go where? We're at a dead end."

45

Karrie raised her hand and pointed. "How are the tires on this SUV?"

"Brand new."

"Good. Keep going down that dirt road. Straight ahead. Do it."

I followed the small dirt road, a tiny artery off the main Old Manor Road. I thought, *Maybe he lived in a secluded mansion off the beaten path with a built-in swimming pool, a hot tub, and a stable.* We continued down the dirt road until we were nearly a mile in. Nailed to a tree, I saw a weathered wooden sign that said "Number 10." I took a sharp curve, traveled about another five hundred feet, and found Freddie's old homestead.

There it was in all its glory. I slammed my SUV into reverse. "Karrie, I'm outta here." Karrie yanked up the emergency brake.

I almost started to cry. It was a huge spooky-looking Gothic Victorian home that would've made the Addams family proud...a crumbling gingerbread mansion decomposing on an overgrown plot of land.

Someone had mowed a narrow path up to the front door, but the surrounding land was an ocean of waist-high weeds. Windows were broken and bed sheets were hung as curtains. Faded yellow paint peeled looked like rotting cheese curls. There were several tires lying around on a large verandah. One particular tire was sliced open, spray-painted hot pink and turned into a planter. The dead flowers and ferns sticking out of the tire-planter added a nice touch. There was a stand-alone industrial fan with large dirty paddles decorating the front porch, right next to an oversized couch with a human-sized indentation on its cushions. I guess Freddie napped on the couch in the summer with the fan blowing on him.

There was a garage that appeared to be collapsing in on itself. In front of one of the garage doors was a lovely manual push mower sticking out of a worn out claw foot bathtub.

Stacks and stacks of newspapers were tied with twine and lined up against the outside of the house. A breeze blew off some loose shingles from the second floor turret.

I just sat there with my mouth open. I closed my eyes, hoping, praying that this dump was an illusion and once I opened my eyes, the nightmare would be over and I would see a really nice house instead. Not happening. I opened my eyes again and looked at my legacy: the Victorian slum that was 10 Old Manor Road in Colts Neck. And now, through an unfortunate twist of fate, I was the new owner of this rat hole.

"Look at this dump, Karrie. What am I going to do with this?"

In her usual calm way, Karrie tried to see the good in the situation. "Let's think for a minute. Large verandah, a few turrets, stained glass windows, and quatrefoil windows. Probably built in the 1800s. Okay, it's a Gothic Victorian house, just one in really bad shape. You can list it as a fixer-upper. Roxie, you may have something here. How much land comes with this property? Do you know?"

"Huh?"

"You're not listening to me."

"Oh I'm listening, alright. Do you hear that sound Karrie? That strange flapping noise? It's the sound of George Washington, Lincoln, and Franklin flapping their arms as they fly out of my wallet. Even if I sell it as is, I probably have to fix it up myself enough to provide the new owner with some basic things, like heat and running water, which I can't afford to do."

I parked the truck and went around to the other side to help Karrie out. As I was doing this, I heard the sound of tires on gravel. It sounded far away but seemed to be getting closer. Then suddenly it stopped.

"Karrie, did you hear that? Sounds like we may have company."

"I don't hear a thing. Shall we go inside and see what treasures lie within?"

I was amazed. Karrie wasn't the least bothered by this whole situation. Not only did I not want to go inside, I wanted to run away to another state and change my name. At that split second, I had made up my mind to renounce this inheritance, as I had no intention of being a Victorian slumlord. I looked at Karrie.

"I don't want to go in. Let's just get out of here."

"Now my dear, I know this isn't the inheritance you wanted, but perhaps there are some things of value inside the house that you can sell. This could be a strange but wonderful gift. However, we won't know until we look around. Buck up, kiddo."

I pulled my SUV onto what was probably the front lawn of the old Victorian. I looked down at the grass I was standing on, and it appeared to have been freshly mowed. Since Freddie wasn't around to do it anymore, if he ever did it at all, I assumed that the town had probably come in and cut the grass. We headed toward a small flight of stairs.

Karrie and I put our hands atop a wobbly balustrade as we walked up the wooden steps that led to the front door. When I reached about the third step, the rotting wood beneath my feet collapsed. Karrie chuckled when she saw me standing on the ground beneath the broken stair.

"Whatever are you doing down there?"

I shrugged my shoulders. "Oh I don't know. Just thought I'd examine the crawl space beneath the house."

"There'll be time to do that later. Let's go inside and see what we can dig out." Karrie extended a hand and helped me to the next step. I reached the doorknob and twisted.

"It's locked. Now what do we do?"

"Isn't it obvious? We break in through a window."

"Wow. Sounds like you've done this before."

"Only if it's an abandoned property," she said with a sweet smile. "Besides, what do you care? You own this dump, I mean this fine Gothic Victorian home."

We went to the back of the house and tried opening a few windows, but they wouldn't budge. It seemed like most of them probably hadn't been opened since the day the house was built. Other windows had too much broken glass around the edges to climb through. But as luck would have it, Karrie finally found a window that she could force open, and we climbed in. We found ourselves in the kitchen, and the first thing I saw was a very old vintage stove. But as I looked around, my heart sank even further. If I thought I had lost my breath when looking at the house from the outside, seeing what was now before me really terrified me.

The Collier brothers would have been proud of Pack Rat Freddie's house. Grocery bags filled with garbage were all over the floor. Ossified food filled the kitchen sink, and a thin layer of dust-like black mold covered almost everything. The walls consisted of wooden paneling that had been painted over with hunter green paint. Newspapers were knee high and piled everywhere. While I searched my purse for Tylenol, I noticed that Karrie was taking notes.

"What are you doing?"

"I am helping you, my dear. I am going to make a list and go through every room to see what you can salvage. Take a look at that beat up box over there." She pointed to a small rotting wooden box with black utensils. From out of her purse, she pulled a tube of bright red lipstick. "Hand me one of those blackened forks."

No way was I going to touch anything in this house. I pulled a tissue from my purse and used it to hand her what looked like a piece of dull, unpolished onyx. She took the lipstick and gently rubbed it over the handle of the fork, then wiped that off with a tissue.

I couldn't believe it. The part of the handle that she had rubbed with the lipstick and polished up was bright white silver. It sparkled. I was amazed; Karrie really did have such a wonderful knowledge of antiques.

"Wow, Karrie. How did you do that?"

"We couldn't afford gold so my first wedding band was silver. My ex-husband used lipstick to polish our wedding band when he was in the Navy. They don't exactly give you silver polish. This was an old trick sailors used. Of course, one wonders which bordello he got the lipstick tube from." She sniffed. "But If this is either sterling or silver plate, it should clean up. And it did, see?" Karrie studied the back of the fork handle closely. "I found a hallmark. This is English sterling." She pointed to a small box. "And it appears that you have more of it. You could definitely resell this at Columbia Meadows or sell it for scrap value. What did I tell you? Treasure amongst trash. Let's keep looking."

I looked at her pristine white slacks. "You picked a great day to wear white." I sighed. "Maybe there is some hope here."

"Think positive. Forget my pants. Just grab that silver. Get a garbage bag this old box is crumbling. I'm going exploring."

I looked around for an empty garbage bag. It shouldn't have been hard to find, and there were plenty of them, but they were all filled to the rim with garbage. I stepped on a banana peel and went flying. Falling backward onto the floor, my head hit a pile of garbage. As I tilted my head slightly to the left, I saw several crushed soda cans.

"I can't believe this place."

Karrie was in the next room and must have heard the big thump from the kitchen as I went down. She came in.

"What are you doing lying around? We have work to do. I just saw some Roseville pottery in another room. We need to grab that stuff."

"Just fell, I'm okay, thanks for asking." I picked myself up from the dirty floor.

"Dear, I'm not worried about you. You're young and rubbery, you'll bounce. Let's go."

I followed Karrie into the living room. She was right. There were several pieces of expensive vintage Clematis Roseville pottery that would do well at Columbia Meadows or on eBay.

"Grab some of that newspaper we saw outside and let's start wrapping."

I went outside and grabbed a pile of newspaper. I broke the twine, and quickly checked the paper for bedbugs. I brought the paper in the house and Karrie started handing me things and ordered me to wrap.

"You know, I kind of feel like this is stealing."

"How can it be stealing if you already own it? You can't kill a dead man and you can't steal your own possessions."

"Yeah, but according to Mr. Queecy, I don't own anything until the will is probated."

"Let's be a little bit logical about this. Fat Freddie has two sisters who are probably really mad that they were left nothing in the will, if they even know he corked off yet. Now if I were them, I'd be coming over here and cleaning the place out before you even got a whiff of the estate. It's our business. People die, we buy."

"I guess you're right, Karrie. It just feels kind of strange."

"My dear Roxie, of course it feels strange. Let's face it. It's not every day one gets to examine the contents of a suburban slum."

As much as I hated to admit it, she was right. I was left this place. Why couldn't I start taking out some of the contents? It wasn't like I was stealing. According to Freddie's last will and testament, all this stuff belonged to me. But with legal issues, the devil is always in the details.

When I was done wrapping the pottery, I moved into an adjacent room. Inside the ankle-deep Lottieris field called a living room, I noticed a lovely mantle clock on top of a fireplace stuffed with bowling pins. In the corner, stacked on top of one another was a group of paintings. Some were framed, some were not. I yelled to Karrie to come into the room.

"Hey, Karrie, we got some artwork in here!"

"Be right there."

When Karrie walked in the room, she was writing. "Roxie, so far I've written down the silver, the Roseville, and I found some interesting Depression glass. The market has kind of dropped out of Depression glass, but I still think you'll be able to move it at Columbia Meadows. What paintings are you talking about?"

"Look over here. They look like something."

"I don't know what you mean when you say that. Something is either a painting or it's not."

"Karrie, I confess, okay? I don't know much about art, classical music, or the opera. In fact, the only opera I ever liked had the Marx Brothers in it."

Karrie smiled. She walked over to the pieces of artwork that were carelessly stacked one on top of another. She began to pick through the artwork. She picked up what looked like an acrylic painting of a daisy. I watched Karrie study the art.

"Looks like a grammar school kid did this one." She picked up the next picture. It was a picture of a banana with a long white beard wearing sunglasses with a palm tree off in the distance. "No accounting for Freddie's bad taste."

"Outsider art, maybe?"

"More like art for the outhouse." She picked up a larger picture. "Don't like the subject matter, but this one is actually well done."

It was a strange painting but clear, crisp, and so well done that it looked like a photograph. It measured twenty-four inches high on one side and about thirty inches wide on the other. In the painting was a tall white candlestick in a lovely silver holder standing on what looked like a kitchen table or cutting board. A dead duck was lying on a white tablecloth with its eyes closed and facing the candlestick; one of duck's legs, even though still attached to its body was tied back with string, and then tacked to a wall. A bowl with a lattice cover lay next to the white duck. While the subject matter didn't appeal to me, a hunter or a duck lover may have found it very interesting.

"I like it," said Karrie. "Amazing really. It almost looks like a photograph. Maybe you could put it in one of those wildlife auctions. You'll probably make some money on it."

"Worth a try, right?"

"I'm going to put this painting, the sterling, and the Roseville in the truck, if you don't mind."

"Wait. Look at this before you go. This is weird."

The next painting was an oil, dark and brooding, with shades of blue, black, and gray. A solitary figure wearing what looked like striped pajamas walked along a barbed wire fence. There was a guard tower and it appeared that the guard in the tower had lowered his gun, pointing it directly at the solitary figure walking alone the distance. The sky was a very strange bluish-gray above the setting sun.

"Hmm. Roxie, this painting has age to it. This looks like a prisoner of war."

"I was thinking the same thing myself. Here, look at this."

I found another painting that had the same horrifying mystique as the first one. It was a series of faces looking through a barbed wire fence. The faces of the people were ghostly pale or had a slightly beige tone to them. They were close together, ragged, and their faces had a hollow look, like they had not eaten in weeks. Again there was a guard tower in the background and the light from the guard tower shined down on the people clinging to the fence.

"These people look like prisoners of war too, Karrie."

"I agree."

"Which war?"

"I'm thinking World War II. But you know, these could be prisoners of war anywhere in the world today. The canvas and the paint look as though they have quite a bit of age to them, though. It's quite yellowed, you see."

"What should we do?"

"I think everything goes with us tonight. If we don't take this stuff, who knows if someone else will?" With that, she grabbed the paintings and left the house, heading out toward the truck.

I stood and stared at my surroundings. I wondered if I should just call one of those 1-800 junk places and have them empty out the entire place after I took what I wanted.

Before I could answer that question, I heard *Crack! Crack! Crack!* The sheetrock in the front wall exploded in pieces and dust. Frantically, I looked at the wall and saw three large holes that weren't there two minutes ago. Almost immediately came the sound of a car tearing off into the distance, away from Freddie's house. Karrie ran back into the house.

"Get down!" Simultaneously we dropped to the floor.

"What's going on?"

"Just stay down!"

I looked wildly in all directions as our bodies lay on piles of Lottieris. Raising a trembling hand, I pointed to the wall. Lined up, perfectly symmetrical, were three bullet holes.

"Someone's trying to kill you," she whispered.

"You think?" I pulled my cell phone out of my jeans. I was shaking so much, I could barely touch the keypad. I was thrilled to hear a voice.

"9-1-1 operator, what is your emergency?"

"I'm at ten Old Manor Road in Colts Neck. Someone just tried to shoot us. We're hiding on the floor."

"Okay, stay with me. Someone is on the way."

Any time I get nervous, the first thing I feel like doing is running to the bathroom. If I did that, I may be a moving target for the shooter. I tried not to think of running water or Niagara Falls.

Five minutes seems like five hours, particularly if you think someone's going to kill you. Karrie and I lay quietly. I was sure we could hear each other breathing. Our hearts pounded. I whispered to her, "When you brought this stuff out to the car, did you see anyone?"

"Not a soul. I didn't hear or see anything."

"I hate to ask this question, but…"

"Yes! I have my hearing aids in!" she snapped.

I looked up and saw headlights and police lights flashing against the wall. Radios crackled and men were talking. The front door opened and cops flooded the inside of Freddie's house, some tripping over garbage that lay on the floor. Finally they made it into the living room.

"Hands where I can see them!" a man's voice yelled.

"It's okay, it's okay. We're the victims here. No need to shoot at us anymore. Somebody's already done that."

More voices on the radio, more men talking, some giving orders. Karrie and I got up from the floor. Somebody yelled about turning on the lights. Somebody hit a wall switch. The lights went on.

The Colts Neck police were first on the scene. Then came Detective Baines, dressed up in his SWAT team best. He looked good.

He sighed. "Why am I not surprised to find you here, Sanchez? I thought you were told to stay away from this house until the estate was probated." Then he turned to look at Karrie. "Mrs. Langston, I'm surprised at you. A woman of your caliber involving yourself in this mess with this one over here," he lectured pointing a finger in my direction.

I watched as Karrie's face flushed bright pink. It was amazing. Detective Baines really had some kind of hold on her. Once again, she started batting eyelashes in his direction and said, "Oh Detective Baines, I'm simply trying to help out this nice young girl. I know she's in a bit of a pickle with this whole estate thing. She and I were just here to catalog some of the items. It was my idea, you see. I thought it might help her with Mr. Queecy."

I watched as he shook a playful finger in her face. "Now, now, Mrs. Langston, we have to be very careful here. Remember there is a homicide investigation going on. I wouldn't want to see anything happen to a fine lady such as yourself."

I rolled my eyes in utter disgust. "And what about me, detective? Aren't you worried that something might actually happen to me?"

He turned to look in my direction. "Nah."

I had to hand it to him. He looked fantastic in his Kevlar vest, badge, and side arm. He looked incredibly sexy. But I was still angry with him.

He started to speak to me, but he was interrupted by another officer who had dug one of the bullets out of the wall and was handing Iceman a plastic bag containing the bullet. I watched as his intense blue eyes studied the bullet inside the bag. He started to walk away, but then he turned and looked back in my direction. He walked back over.

"Look, I don't have time to give you a ballistics lesson. Let me just tell you this. This is a .50 caliber bullet. The fact that you're not dead isn't a happy accident."

"What?" I felt the color draining from my face.

"Let's just say that those three shots were warning shots. People using these kinds of bullets generally don't miss their target. I'm going to give you a piece of advice. Don't come back here."

Now I got indignant. "Really? Really? How can I not come back here where I own all, all this?" I opened my arms to the slum around me.

"Sanchez, if you remember from the meeting…"

"Stop call me Sanchez! It's Ms. Sanchez to you!" I was really tired of this guy ordering me around. "Or else I'm going to call you Iceman!"

"Funny you should say that. That was my nickname in the Army." He gave me a boyish grin, as though I had caught his hand in the cookie jar. He looked at me with piercing eyes, but his tone of voice softened a little bit. "I'm sorry. Maybe I've been too abrupt, but

I have a dead body in the morgue and I'm trying to figure out how it got there. You know, Farmingdale isn't exactly the murder capital of New Jersey."

"Not to bring up a sore subject, but when do you intend to release the body? I have to bury him."

"The coroner's finished with the report. We'll probably release the body to you sometime tomorrow. I called his two sisters."

"And?"

"They told me that they would simply pay their respects at the funeral. They wanted no part of the process. My recollection from our meeting the other day is that as the third beneficiary, you drew the short straw."

"Oh great." I sighed. "I know how to arrange funerals. I did it for both my parents, I just didn't think I'd be doing it for complete stranger."

He put his hand on my shoulder. For a minute, a look of sympathy melted those his handsome deity-like features into someone more human. I thought he wanted to say a few kind words, but that would've been too much for him. Instead he just said, "Good luck" and left.

I chased after him. "Wait! You just told me I can't take anything out of here. I have to have a suit to bury him in. Can I at least look around and find some clothes for him?"

He sighed. His annoyance was evident. "I'll go upstairs with you. You look for something to bury him in. Maybe you can find that suit he wore in the video."

A voice from the next room cheerfully added, "If worse comes to worst, we can always wrap him up like a fish. There's plenty of newspaper."

"Karrie!" I yelled. "Can you please stop with the dead jokes?"

Iceman laughed.

I wasn't amused. It was Wednesday. I could hardly wait.

CHAPTER 6

I was never really much good at this death stuff. Oh sure, we all have to go sometime. But burying a next-to-complete stranger? Low on my bucket list, like getting poison ivy in my armpits, or hanging from a clothesline by my eyebrows. This was going to be a disaster.

I made arrangements at the Freehold Funeral Home for Freddie, asking, begging, for the shortest wake possible. If I could've had a drive-through funeral and dropped him in the ground within an hour, that would've been perfectly fine with me.

I arranged a one-night wake with a seven p.m. to nine p.m. viewing. I convinced Mr. Queecy to advance me some money and the rest I put on my credit card. I had to call the credit card company and ask for a slight extension on my credit because of an emergency. They were actually sympathetic and gracious. After the arrangements were made, I contacted Karrie.

She put up a notice on the Columbia Meadows Flea Market bulletin board, and I reached out to a local Masonic Lodge. I was told by a lodge member that they would send over a brother Mason to do a brief prayer. I ordered a large funeral spray that had a "Dear Friend" banner spread across bunches of crowded red carnations in the shape of a heart. The ever-faithful Karrie met me at six-thirty to help me make sure the place was set up properly.

As usual, she looked elegant and lovely, until she removed her coat. The view was blinding.

"Red? Are you kidding me? You wear a cherry red suit to a wake?"

"Red's a festive color for any occasion," she tittered. "Honestly, for a young girl you worry too much. Freddie can't see me. He's dead, remember, Sweetie?"

I slapped my palm to my forehead so hard, I thought my eyeballs would pop out the back of my head. "I can't believe this. It's a wake. You're wearing a red suit. Do you know what we say in Spanish culture? *Yo bailo en la tuba en un vestido rojo.* I dance on your grave in a red dress! Wearing red is an insult to the dead and their family. Where I come from people get knifed over stuff like this! What were you thinking?"

"We're not in San Juan and I don't have time to change. Ah look, mourners have arrived. Remember to be gracious no matter how annoying."

At seven o'clock sharp, Freehold Funeral Home opened its doors. As I watched the various Columbia Meadows characters shuffle in, a single thought ran through my head: *The circus has just come to town.*

One by one they lined up in front of the guest book. Fishy was the first one in, wearing his best business casual plaid flannel shirt and a tie that looked like it had some confetti stuck to it. Lottie came in wearing a short black miniskirt with an elegant Hermes bag so big, you could have stored a dead elephant in it. Attached to her other arm was her latest conquest, a chatty, frail seventy five plus gentleman. Bug Eye was dressed entirely in black from head to toe with a matching beret. JJ's braids flowed along with a caftan. Her makeup was elegant. She was the first to greet me.

"So sorry for your loss, my girl."

"Thanks. More of a loss than you can imagine."

"You be doin' de work of de angels, buryin' a stranger. God will bless you twice over." She put her arm around me. "May I go in to see 'im?"

"Sure, JJ."

"I wish to do little bit of prayin' on 'im. His soul is quite restless, you know."

I leaned over and whispered in her ear. "He's still walking around. Is he here?"

"Um-hmm. Right behind you." She raised an eyebrow. "He keeps sayin' something about Aunt Terry's. Do you have an aunt named Terry that be 'avin' something of his?"

I gulped. "Do you mean Antares?"

"Yes, yes. That is what he's sayin'." JJ cocked her head. "Like de stars? Antares?"

I nodded, thinking, *this is too weird. There's no way she could have known what he said in that video.*

"Yes."

"Okay, my girl. You take care of de people. Let me talk to 'im. I have influence wit de dead." She walked up to the casket and bowed her head.

I stood frozen as my emotions went numb. There was no time to analyze my feelings, so I just did the best I could to be polite. I stepped away from the door. Karrie was talking to someone standing near the funeral spray. I sat down and made myself comfortable in the front of the room.

Macoun Ferguson came in the door. He sat down next to me and patted my hand. "I am here on behalf of the Blackwood and Pynchard firm," he announced. "However, I did bring my own Mass card for you. It's from Mother and me. She would've made it here tonight to pay her respects, but she's little under the weather."

"Under the weather? God bless her, she's ninety-one years old. It's okay, Mac. I didn't expect her to come. But I do appreciate you coming here tonight."

"This must be hard for you, I mean, you not knowing the man and all."

"I could've never predicted that sitting next to someone at a flea market would result in a homicide and then burying the corpse. I really didn't know him well."

"Police have any leads. Any leads at all?"

"Mac, if they do, I'm sure I'd be the last to know."

"I see. As Lewis Carroll said in *Alice in Wonderland*, 'curiouser and curiouser'." I could see he was a bit nervous and really didn't know what to say to me.

"Mac, did you know–"

"I heard through Pynchard. Someone shot at you when you were at Freddie's house. This thing's getting dangerous."

"Yeah." I could see that Mac was thinking very seriously. He looked nervous and concerned. At least someone was. I told him, "They yanked a .50 caliber bullet out of the wall."

"That's long-range sniper stuff, I think. Read about it in a book once."

"Great. Yeah, three bullets fired to be exact." I sat back. "How did you know?"

"Oh, Pynchard mentioned it in the coffee break room at the firm. He overheard you talking."

"How did he say it?"

"Roxie, he said it with all his usual warmth and sincerity."

"I bet he was sorry the shooter missed."

Poor Mac! He liked Pynchard as much as I did, but he never said anything bad about anyone, even people he didn't like who didn't like him. He was just a polite gentleman. My remark made him look like he wanted to crawl out of his white shirt that he had worn for a week straight. "Unfortunately,…you know how he is."

"Indeed. About as warm as an Artic breeze in January I expect," Mac blushed, his cheeks turning bright red. I grabbed his hand. "Listen, thanks so much for coming. And thank you for the Mass card. I must go and see the rest of the folks here, be polite, and all that other good stuff. By the way, I couldn't get to your shirt this week. I'm sorry."

"Of course, I understand. It's okay though. I bought a new one."

"So I guess that means you own three shirts now?"

"I'm back down to two. I had to retire one. Hole in the elbow." We laughed.

When he left, I went over to the coffin to take a look at Freddie. He looked pretty darn good. Oh, great. Now I sounded like my sister when she goes to funerals. Angela would always comment on how good or bad people looked in the coffin. I didn't understand how anyone could look good. You're dead, pushing up daisies. That can't be good.

I had to admit, though, Freddie looked peaceful. Now I wished someone could figure out who killed the poor son of a gun.

I watched as Karrie made the rounds. She sat with Bug Eye for a bit, as she kept trying to dodge Fishy. She finally plopped down next to Lottie and her new octogenarian boyfriend. More people entered. Red Hawk had come in, unnoticed at first, and he sat quietly in the back of the funeral parlor. Then much to my surprise, twenty-five jacketed men came in.

Karrie walked over to me. "Oh, these must be Freddie's Masonic brothers. They certainly seem to be the right age."

"They all look old to me."

The jackets seemed to be pretty well organized, and as they filed in, they sat down on chairs in the parlor. The man leading the Masonic parade approached me.

"Good evening, Ms. Sharona. My name is Justin Petri. Thank you for burying our brother Frederick. Had you not taken the responsibility, we would have done it. I don't think he had any family."

"It's Sanchez, and yes, he has two sisters, but I understand he didn't want to give them the job, and they didn't want it anyway." I sighed. "But on a more positive note, he did want a Masonic prayer said, and I appreciate that you are doing this." I wondered if I should have told him that I really enjoyed this job as much as I enjoyed sticking pins in my arm. "Thank you for coming."

"When you're ready, let me know. It won't be a traditional Masonic funeral, but we can make do. Then my Masonic brothers and I will be on our way."

I turned to look at him. "Mr. Petri, what was he like?"

The old Mason smiled. "What do you mean?"

"Look, I really didn't know this guy. I mean, he had a table next to me in a flea market. I know he was kind of messy, could be kind of cheap, and sold a lot of crap. What I'm asking you is this: what was Freddie like? As a person, I mean. You probably saw him a little differently."

The gentleman sat back and look thoughtful. "You're kind of right. In the Lodge, he was notorious for hoarding pencils and little bits of paper he thought he could reuse. I really don't know why he collected the way he did. Just a little eccentric I guess. But he was also very generous to other people in need. When he knew someone needed an operation, he would give a large donation., anonymously. His heart was good, I think. Did you ever see his house?"

"Yes. I went to visit his house recently."

Mr. Petri looked a little nervous. "Was there a lot of gar-"

"You have no idea. I was literally knee-deep in stuff I'd rather not talk about." As I had this conversation, my thoughts went back to tripping and falling on my back into a pile of filthy junk, half-eaten things, and rotten produce.

"Ms., ah, Sarona, if there's anything we at the Liberty Tree Lodge can do, here's my card. Feel free to call me."

"Do you guys rent backhoes? I could use one to empty his kitchen." The old gentleman laughed, patted me on the shoulder and stepped away. All the jacketed men came up one by one, shaking my hand and offering their condolences. At the tail end of the line was someone I only half expected to see. In a way, I was almost relieved to see Detective Baines.

The man had no right to look this good, even at a wake. He carried a windbreaker with a tightly knit thermal underneath. I couldn't help but look at those arms, like chiseled marble, those terribly strong arms. But I slapped myself back into reality once he opened his mouth.

He smiled. "Sanchez, good evening. Oh, I'm sorry. I mean Ms. Sanchez."

"Good evening, Detective Baines. So nice of you to drop by and see me."

"I'm not here to see you. But I am here to see who's here to see you. I don't have to tell you that sometimes murderers come back to see their handiwork." He offered me one of those chiseled arms. "Let's go up and pay old Freddie our respects, okay?"

A lump rose in my throat. I grabbed his arm and we started walking up to the coffin. But I suddenly stopped in my tracks. My knees felt wobbly. I broke free from his arm, turned around and sat down, gesturing him to join me.

"You okay? You're not going to faint or something like that. Don't worry. I won't catch you," he grinned.

"That's okay, already hit the ground once this week." I mustered up in a weak voice. "I know this is going to sound really idiotic, but what did he die from?"

"Fairly straightforward kill. Knife to the chest. Severed the aorta. He bled out." He turned and gave me those blue eyes. "I have a question for you."

"Yeah?"

"You know anything about antique knives?"

"If you're talking about hunting knives, I can put you in touch with a guy at the flea market who knows hunting knives, military knives, samurai swords, that sort of stuff. If you're talking about kitchen knives, I may be able to help you with some of that. If not me, my friend Karrie can."

"Good. I'd like to talk to you or Mrs. Langston about this sometime." He looked around at the people in the funeral parlor who were coming in. "Place is packed. I think some people want to come and talk to you. I'm going to sit in the back. Feel free to ignore me. Like you usually do." He winked. He got up from the chair and went to the back of the room. I stood up and was headed over to talk to another flea market vendor, but before I could sit down again, a woman stood in front of me, blocking my way.

She was extremely well dressed, but if it weren't for her expensive clothing, coiffed hair, and makeup, you'd expect to find her wearing a muumuu, smoking a skinny cigarette, and picking her teeth in public. She had jet black hair like Freddie. And like Freddie's hair, the natural jet black pigment had walked off her scalp years ago. As I looked at her face, I thought I recognized her.

"Hi, can I help you?"

"I don't want your help. You probably know who I am. I'm Jule Mustergrave."

"I'm sorry for your loss."

She looked bored. "Thanks, I guess. Death happens. Don't worry. I have no interest in talking to any of these people. This is your show."

I was floored. I didn't know what to say. But I suddenly had a feeling this was not going to be an easy conversation.

"Just for the record," stated Mrs. Mustergrave, "my sister and I do appreciate you burying our brother Selwyn."

When she said "Selwyn," I giggled unabashedly.

"Did I say something funny, Ms. Sanchez?"

"I'm sorry Mrs. Mustergrave. I only knew your brother as Freddie."

"*We* only knew him as Selwyn."

"I see." The tone of this witch's voice irritated me. I really didn't care if she knew him as Mickey Mouse.

"I guess you are one of those flea market peddlers he used to hang around with. I don't know." She sighed. " I'll just never understand why Selwyn wanted to hang around with people of that ilk. We come from a very old family." She looked around the room. "I mean, just look at this bunch. A motley crew if there ever was one."

"Oh, I don't know, Mrs. Mustergrave. They're not so bad. Maybe Freddie just didn't want to hang around with a sourball who looked down her nose at people. Now if you have anything you want to ask me, ask, but as you can see, there's a parlor full of people I have to talk to."

Mrs. Mustergrave gave me one of those smiles that only the Grinch who stole Christmas could've loved, pure villain with a twist of sinister. "I wouldn't get too comfortable with my brother's money. We do intend on challenging the will. I don't know what kind of influence you had on him or those psychotic Shriners he hung around with, but that money is not yours. My sister and I are his family. Not you."

I had a moment to gather my thoughts, none of which were any good. I envisioned myself driving a Lamborghini at breakneck speed and using this broad as a hood ornament. I could take her in a street fight. But wait, we lived in civilized society. People didn't do those kinds of things. I just couldn't believe how nasty she was. And if the other sister was like this one, I completely understood why Freddie had left the gruesome twosome a whopping ten cents to be split between them. Believe me, I wasn't entirely convinced they were worth a nickel a piece.

"Mrs. Mustergrave, I'm really sorry, but I have to go speak with other people who came here tonight. I can give you the name of my lawyer if you like."

She gave me that smug grin again. "Don't need it. Edward Pynchard went to law school with my husband. The four of us had dinner last week." She turned and started to walk away." What is that phrase? Ah yes, 'See you in Court?'"

"Umm, Mrs. Mustergrave?"

"Yes?"

"Mrs. Mustergrave, I just want to let you know that you look a lot like Freddie. Except that he was right. You do have a better mustache." I reached into my purse and grabbed a nickel. "Oh, and here's your half of the inheritance Freddie left you. Don't spend it all in one place." I flung the nickel at her. Her face looked like it was going to explode.

With that, I turned to greet the next mourner.

****

It seemed like the longest two hours in the history of modern man. I mean, I never liked wakes to begin with, but I liked them even less under these circumstances. The only good thing about this was that I saw many people from the flea market, and they were actually very nice. Okay, so they were odd sorts, but they had hearts big enough to care about a fellow vendor.

Lottie and her latest love interest sat next to me. Lottie was an attractive woman in her youth and she was still really nice looking now. What she was doing with Father Time was anybody's guess. There she was, a gorgeous fifty-something, petite with an hourglass figure and a lion's mane of blond hair, with a flawless face. And there he was: pencil neck, skinny like a twig, with deep-set tiny little eyes. This man was a piece of animated beef jerky. He must've had a ton of money because there was no way Lottie would be clocking any time with this guy otherwise.

"Honey, you're earning some big brownie points in heaven. Oh, I'd like to introduce you to Rob, Rob Hatchett. Rob, or should I say Judge Hatchett, has retired from the bench. Rob, this is my dear friend, Roxie Sanchez."

He cupped a hand to his ear. "Wh-what? What did you say?"

Lottie raised her voice. "I said, this is my friend, Roxie Sanchez."

He shook his head slightly. "Your cousin?"

"No, Rob," she yelled. "My friend from the flea market!"

At this point, the entire funeral parlor had come to a hushed silence. Everyone looked at the three of us attempting to have a conversation with a deaf man. Out of desperation, I stuck out my hand.

"Hi, I'm Roxie Sanchez. Nice to meet you, Judge Hatchett."

The elderly gentleman smiled and nodded. He looked at Lottie and me, announcing that he needed the men's room. Then he got up and hobbled away.

"Lottie, don't you think he's a little old for you?"

"He's perfect. I get a diamond bracelet or a Hermes crocodile purse, and all I have to do is have sex with him once a month."

"That's way too much information, way too much."

"Any luck with finding out who killed our Freddie?"

"If there's information out there, Lottie, they're not telling me."

"I have something for you." She reached into her Hermes bag. "It's from all of us at Columbia Meadows. Rumor had it that you were going to get stuck picking up the entire tab for this shindig, so we took up a collection. Hope that it helps in some small way. Oh, and I also want to tell you that the Marias can't make it tonight but send their condolences."

"Oh, did they get that job cleaning out that mansion in Rumson?"

"Yeah. They're sending a lot of money back to Mexico for their families. They're really strapped for cash. Had to start unloading tonight."

"I completely understand. And thank everyone for coming and doing the donation thing. That was really sweet of you all."

"Hey, we're all in this together. I mean, let's face it, Columbia Meadows is like a club. Of course, it's a club nobody wants to join, but we still care about each other."

Right then, Lottie's old judge returned to the room. I watched the old man's eyes light up when he saw her.

"Darling, over here," she purred.

As I looked across the room, I saw Mr. Petri trying to get my attention. "Lottie, listen. I think the Mason guy wants to do his prayer for Freddie. I better go over to him."

I got up and walked over to Mr. Petri. He asked me if now was a good time for the prayer. I nodded yes before going to stand in front of Freddie's casket.

"Everyone, everyone can I have your attention please? Mr. Petri is from the Masonic Liberty Tree Lodge. Freddie, as you know, was a Mason, and while he didn't want a full Masonic funeral, he did want his brothers to say a few words. Mr. Petri?"

The old leader and his fez-wearing army came forward. Karrie sat on the main couch in front of the little Masonic parade. I joined her. I watched as Mr. Petri dug in his coat pocket for his reading glasses.

"Thank you all for coming tonight. As you know, our brother, Freddie, has reached the end of his earthly toils. The brittle thread which bound him to earth has been severed, and his liberated spirit has winged its flight to the unknown world. The silver cord is loosed; the golden bowl is broken; the pitcher is broken at the fountain; and the wheel is broken at the cistern. The dust has returned to the earth as it was, and the spirit has returned to God who gave it..."

Karrie gently tugged on my sleeve. "Do you think they're going to yack all night?"

"S-s-s-sh," I whispered. "They were nice enough to come do this."

"I'm sure that's very nice, but do you know how long these Masonic ceremonies take? My ex-husband was a Mason. They could be babbling for hours."

"They won't be. They can't be. This place closes at nine. Anyway, funeral mass at St. Robert Bellarmine's will be quick."

"I thought he didn't want a mass. He was Catholic?"

"He is now. Besides, I wanted to give him something spiritual. We do a quick trip to the cemetery and then to the American Hotel in Freehold for the repast."

"Who's paying for all this?"

"Freddie and me. Mr. Queecy released some money to me for the funeral service. Now be quiet for five minutes, will you?"

Thanks to Karrie's chattering, I missed the entire prayer. I glanced up at the clock and it was already after eight o'clock. In about forty-five minutes, this whole thing would be over. I couldn't wait.

JJ and Red Hawk came up to me after the prayers had finally ended. Red Hawk was the one who spoke first.

"I just wanted to give my condolences and tell you that Freddie's spirit is very restless."

I rolled my eyes. "Yes, I know. He's unhappy."

"He wants you to find out who killed him."

"You know, I'd really like to do that. But I think that's why they have police officers."

Red Hawk looked very serious. "He was killed for a reason. I think all you need to do is find out the reason and then you'll find the killer."

"Isn't that how the police figure out most murders? Reason? Motive? Opportunity? Whatever. I'll do what I can. But I'm not a police officer."

Red Hawk smiled. "Spirit will guide you."

JJ chimed in. "Listen to de Red man here. He know what he's talkin' about, sista."

I looked at the two of them and thought about how nice it was of them to actually come to this fiasco. But I just didn't consider that I would somehow be responsible for solving some guy's murder. Solving crimes just didn't appeal to me.

****

We had a quickie church mass the next morning. We went to Heavenly Rest Cemetery where a few words were said, and he was lowered into the ground. I had on my black dress from last night. Karrie wore another red suit with a big stovepipe hat. Many of the same people who came last night stood quietly at the graveside. I looked toward the back of the crowd and saw Ying in his cook's outfit. He smiled and waved.

When all was done, I invited everyone back to the American Hotel for a luncheon. Knowing the Columbia Meadows crowd, they wouldn't pass up free food and booze. Detective Baines didn't show up. I was disappointed, but it was a full house. Toward the end of the meal, I proposed a toast.

"Here's to Freddie, a fellow flea marketer and a good soul. I'm sure if he were here, he'd be joining us in a Scotch or two."

Karrie yelled from the back of the table. "Or the whole bottle and then he'd fall flat on his dead drunk a–" The crowd laughed, but I wasn't amused.

"God rest him!" I interrupted. "To Freddie!"

The crowd replied, "To Freddie!"

****

By the time Karrie and I had made it back to my apartment, it was past three o'clock. Sitting at my kitchen table held together with spit and gum, we reviewed the bills from the funeral and wake. I started writing checks.

"Gee, Karrie, look at these bills. How can anyone afford to croak these days?"

"Most people have burial insurance for this sort of thing. Or else they're like Freddie with lots of money."

"Thank you for helping out between last night and today. I really appreciate it."

"No worries. I guess you've forgiven me for wearing the red suit then?"

"Look, Karrie, I don't know what to say. It was a terrible thing that he ruined your basket. But I'm sure he didn't mean it. He was drunk at the time."

"I'm over it. He's gone. That beautiful basket and six thousand dollars is gone. Can't cry over spilled milk." She handed me the guest-book from the funeral parlor. "You'll need this for thank you notes. Look at this. I don't know if it means anything. There was a guest at the wake that wasn't from Columbia Meadows."

"Anyone we know?"

Karrie opened the book. She went down the names, addresses and signatures of all the attendees. She pointed to a name with no address. A chill went down my spine all the way into my toes.

I couldn't believe it. Written in very large letters and very dark ink was the name Avi Antares.

"Roxie, isn't that the name mentioned in the video will?"

I gulped. "Ye-yeah. That was it."

Oh great. It was going to be another sleepless night.

CHAPTER 7

I had to take off Thursday and Friday for Freddie's wake. However, because of the firm's policy, I was unable to use any personal time, since Freddie was not a family member. This decision was, of course, made by Pynchard, who had no sympathy for my situation. So I was forced to take days off without pay in order to prepare for Freddie's funeral and burial. Mac recommended that I bill the estate for my lost wages, but that seemed kind of a crass thing to do.

In order to make up the difference, I was hoping to have a good Saturday and Sunday at Columbia Meadows. Karrie and I had our usual tables, and we had a new neighbor parked in Freddie's space. It was amazing. Freddie's body wasn't even cold and his table on the midway was already rented out to a new vendor. But after seeing my new neighbor, I wasn't entirely unhappy.

He had dark olive skin, and his thick chestnut brown hair was shoulder length and wavy. He drove a brand new pickup truck. In the truck's bed, I saw carefully packed, expensive-looking antique clocks and vases. This stuff was really nice and looked really old. I thought we would have some pretty stiff competition. Didn't know what his prices were, but his stuff looked pretty darn good. I looked at Karrie, and I right away noticed that she gave him the old stink eye. That green-eyed monster called jealousy had just arrived on the scene.

"Just looking from here, I think all those vintage clocks are reproductions."

"Not sure. They could be. Can't tell. I'm going to go over and introduce myself. Care to join me?"

"Not at all."

I walked over to his table. *My, my!*

He wasn't very tall but he had an incredible body. Different from Detective Baines, yet probably in as great shape as his. He had a couple of tattoos on his arm, and they were in a language I didn't recognize. He was getting out the last of the clocks when he finally caught my stare.

"Mademoiselle, is there something I can show you?" he asked.

Hey, no one's ever called me that before. "Hi, I'm Roxie."

He gave me an easy smile. "So I'm the new guy to the neighborhood, yes?"

"New people come and go all the time. I was admiring your stuff."

"Is there something I can show you?"

"No, I'm not buying right now. Have too much inventory of my own that I have to move."

He came around the table. I looked at his face. His features were a bit hard, but they were incredibly strong. I noticed he had a slight scar above his eye and very dark kissable lips. I was attracted to him in a strange way. But then again, I've been attracted to a lot of men who broke my heart, particularly the good-looking, bad boy types. Something about men who looked like they had a touch of mischief in them intrigued me.

"You know, my darling, you can never have enough inventory. People love to buy. And I will give you a great deal on anything you want because you're such a nice-looking woman."

That remark alone made me want to buy something whether I needed it or not. Listening to him speak, I heard a slight accent, but I couldn't figure it out. Around Columbia Meadows you heard lots of accents: Spanish, Italian, German, Russian, French, and the ever-popular Brooklynese. This accent was slightly different, nothing I'd ever heard before. I couldn't put my finger on it. Nor could I figure out this guy's background. I decided to stop playing around and just ask him outright.

"What's your name?"

"David Williams." He stuck out a calloused hand.

I smiled. "You know, you don't look like any David Williams I've ever seen."

He gave me a big grin and leaned into me. "That's because you never met a David like me."

I was really enjoying flirting with my new friend until Karrie yelled to me.

"Oh missy! We have a few customers over here."

"I'm sorry, David, I have to go back to my table. My friend, Karrie, gets a little impatient when she's left alone."

He folded his arms. "I plan to be here awhile, Ms. Roxie. I think that you and I will get to know each other much better soon."

"I hope so."

As I began to turn away, David gestured me back. He put an arm around me, pulled me close, and whispered in my ear. "I want to let you in on a little secret. The 19th Century clocks?"

"Yes?"

"They are reproductions. I keep the real ones at home."

"Okay. Good to know." I went back to my table. As usual, Karrie was a bit miffed that I had taken so long talking to the new vendor. However, I could see that she was eager to know what, if anything, I found out about his merchandise and how it compared to ours.

"So besides the flirting, did you get any good info?"

I rolled my eyes. "Yes. The clocks are repros."

"Whew." Karrie put an index finger to her chin. "If the clocks are reproductions, then I guess it's a safe bet that the rest of those Chinese temple jars are repros, too. What do they say? False in one, false in all?"

"He seems like a nice person, Karrie."

"Forget nice. He's competition. But we have the better merchandise. The old genuine stuff. That's what people want. I mean if you want a nice repro, you could go anywhere for that."

"Anywhere? Anywhere like a flea market?"

"Change of subject. I've been doing a little research."

Now that was scary. As I thought about Karrie doing research, to me that meant she was going in for the kill. She was onto something. She didn't waste time researching things that she thought had no value.

"What kind of research? The paintings?"

"Yes. And some of the line drawings."

"What line drawings?"

"The ones I took from Freddie's house."

"Wait a minute. I thought you took the paintings. Remember I told you, I'm not even supposed to be in that house. Line drawings? Whose line drawings? Who? Who?"

"Hoo! hoo! Hoo! hoo! You sound like an owl." She laughed.

Right now I wished I was an owl. Then I'd be asleep because it's daytime, and oh yes, then at night I could just fly away and look for mice.

"Didn't mean to ruffle your feathers dear. But that one painting with the duck? It has quite a bit of history to it. When we're done with this place, let's stop for lunch and I'll give you all the details."

While I was talking to Karrie, I noticed that a woman had shown interest in a vintage salt and pepper shaker set that was made of opaque green ribbed glass called jadeite. I had a sixty dollar price tag on the set, but I was always willing to negotiate. I could see from the look on this woman's face that she really wanted them.

"How much?"

"Sixty, but I could do a little bit better."

I was trying to figure out from the way this woman had sized up the situation if she was a dealer or just a plain old buyer. She picked up the shakers, examining each one as though it was going to be sold at Sotheby's. When her exhaustive examination was over, she turned to me.

"That is way overpriced. I'll offer you twenty-five dollars."

Truth be told, I didn't have that much in them. I probably could have sold them for thirty or forty bucks. I was just about to make a counter offer, but then Karrie cut in.

"I'm sorry, ma'am," she said with a smile. "We have very nice things here, but if you want garbage you can always go to the next table."

I watched as an angry red-faced woman put down the shakers and walked away. There went my sale of merchandise I had been unable to unload for the past year. Money on two fat legs walked away. Karrie just stood there smiling as though she was the cat with not one, but two canaries in her mouth.

"Was that really necessary? I mean, you told me I should work people for money, and that's what I was trying to do. Why did you have to insult the woman?"

"Those two salt shakers are vintage jadeite from the 1930s. Any idiot can see they're all original. You don't get fine antiques for free. This is a flea market, not a *free* market."

"Yeah, but Karrie, come on. If people wanted truly fine antiques, they'd be at Blake and Faraday's or Sotheby's."

"Are you saying those old shakers aren't fine pieces? I sold them to you, remember?"

Now it all made sense. She was mad because she thought that I was going to give away something at a cheap price that she had sold to me steeply discounted. Her feelings were hurt.

"Karrie, I have had a great deal of respect for everything you've sold to me and all the stuff you taught me. I wasn't going to give them away at a ridiculous price. I think my price may have been too high given this market. People just don't have the kind of money they used to."

I watched as she wrung her hands. Karrie always did that when she was nervous. "Sorry. Maybe all this murder stuff has really gotten to me a little bit. When today's over, I should just go home."

I felt kind of bad. "Nah. Don't go home. I need a drink. So do you."

****

When the day was finally over, we packed up quickly. Karrie and I went to a local watering hole called the Court Jester in downtown Freehold. The Jester is a great little place for burgers and other kinds of meals. It was also a watering hole for the local Monmouth County Bar Association. At any given time, the place was crawling with either lawyers or cops. I wouldn't have to worry about being mugged when I was sitting at the Jester. Certainly no one would kill me there. I hoped.

The day had been a little tight, but I still managed to walk away with three hundred fifty dollars. I think Karrie did about the same. She was sipping a nice cool rosé, while I ordered a Guinness Stout. When we finally got down to talking about the art from Freddie's house, she became very serious.

"We may have a problem with some of the art."

"Let me guess. It's garbage. Are you telling that I nearly got shot for something I could buy at Walmart for ten bucks."

She smiled. "Well, that's not quite it. It's a bit more complicated."

"God, I hate when you say that. How complicated?"

"How does stolen art sound?"

I suddenly felt the color draining from my face. I've always prided myself on living a clean life, no drugs, only an occasional glass of wine, and a joyful romp with a good-looking man when time permitted. I've never stolen a thing in my life, and I was appalled at the fact that I was in possession of something that clearly wasn't mine.

"Freddie had hot art?" I asked, sipping my beer.

"Well, dear, not in the sense of attractive 'hot', like the way young people talk about actors or singers being 'sexy hot.' I was thinking more in line with the term, oh you know, stolen?"

I gagged. "We-we ha-ave to report this."

"If we report it, people are going to wonder how you came about getting it. I found a site called artlost-dot-com. That painting with a duck?"

"The ugly one? The one that looks like a photograph?"

"Yes, that one. It apparently came from some estate in England and has been missing since 1990. It is called *The White Duck* and was painted by Jean-Baptiste Oudry."

"How did Freddie get it? I mean, this is a man who sells broken wrenches. Now you're telling me he owns a piece of famous stolen art worth a million bucks?"

"Try about eleven million. It's a sixteenth century painting, for God's sake."

"I think we need to call Detective Baines. I mean, that would be a motive for killing Freddie."

Karrie became indignant. "I am not so much interested in who killed Freddie and why. But I am concerned that you're in possession of an eleven million dollar painting that was stolen over twenty years ago. And I haven't even got to the etchings or the line drawings yet. Wait till I tell you about those!"

There went my hand again. My palm smacked into my forehead, almost knocking my eyeballs out of my head and onto the table next to us. "What etchings?"

"Oh, didn't I tell you? Oh foo, it must've skipped my mind. I removed a book from the Colts Neck house that contained etchings from a stolen sketchbook by – a-a-h, oh dear, what's that fella's name again? I think he might be Italian. Name some Italian artists."

"Who are we talking about here? Da Vinci?"

She shook her head. "No, wasn't him. I would've known that name."

"Botticelli?"

"Nope."

"Dante Alighieri?"

"No. Started with a P. Piccadilly, Pecorino, Picante?"

"Karrie, pecorino is a type of cheese. Picante is a hot salsa. If this guy was an artist and a part-time taco or cheese salesman, I doubt if any of his art would be worth very much."

"No, no, no," she argued. "The name will come to me." Suddenly her eyes lit up. "I know! The guy's name was Picasso."

"He was Spanish!"

"Oh, Spaniards, Italians, Greeks, they're all Mediterranean. What's the difference? Freddie had Picasso's sketchbook. Stolen years ago, apparently."

"Karrie, what am I going to with this stuff? I mean, if it's stolen, I can't keep it. I can't sell it. I'm stuck."

"Let's think about this. If the art is stolen may be there some kind of reward. But I guess the real issue is how you obtained the stolen art."

"I'm going to call Baines. I'm not comfortable with any of this."

****

I was glad the day was over. I made enough money at the flea market to pay this month's bills and even have a little left over. But I was still stuck in an uncomfortable situation. I just buried a murder victim and inherited stolen art. I would have to let my law firm know, and this made me nervous. I had a feeling that somehow Edward Pynchard would think I had something to do with stolen art. And how could I forget this lawsuit that was hanging out there by Jule Mustergrave and her sister in a will contest? And during the course of all of this insanity, someone had tried to shoot me using .50 caliber bullets.

I really needed a rescue, but whether anyone was up for the task was anybody's guess. I had the curse of my own bad luck.

Crazy thoughts kept running through my mind. I kept having fantasies about my emotional rescue.

I was hanging off the edge of a cliff by my fingers, expecting Liam Neeson, Vin Diesel, or that big blond guy who plays Thor to save me from bad guys chasing me with automatic weapons. Just when I have the visuals of warm, strong biceps yanking me up from the edge of the cliff and kicking the crap out of my attackers, a balding, bent little man with fragile hair appears. He starts talking to the gunmen about his hemorrhoids and how the peppers he ate last night at this terrible yet swank restaurant in Soho kept repeating on him. He asked the gunmen if they have anti-acids handy. The gunmen look confused, shrug their shoulders, but proceed to reload their weapons.

My hero. Finger by sweaty finger, I allow myself to slip off the rocky cliff. My body hurls into the rushing waters below because I would rather die than listen to him.

A raving beauty queen I am not. My next fantasy involves going for a beauty treatment at a Beverly Hills salon, I demand the operator who does the makeup for Angelina Jolie. She's not available so I wind up with a cut rate cosmetologist. I leave the salon looking like Elsa Lanchester from the Bride of Frankenstein. I've always said if it weren't for my bad luck, I'd have no luck at all.

As I lay in bed, all of these thoughts kept rolling through my head. I kept tossing and turning, trying to talk myself into sleep. I put on some meditation music. I made sure I was in a completely dark room. I tried to think happy thoughts, get to my happy place. But it was at that moment I realized I didn't have a happy place to run to.

I was on the run from a killer. I had stolen art in my possession, and I was facing a lawsuit for an estate I really didn't even want. I rolled from one side to the other, putting a pillow over my head. I needed to sleep, but nothing was happening. I screamed into the pillow.

At midnight, the sleep fairies came dancing on tiny Cabernet legs. As I finished the last gulp, I thought how rotten the world would be without good wine. My body finally relaxed with that nice comfortable heaviness that starts off a good sleep. Comfortable, completely thoughtless about anything, I started to drift off.

Then I heard a sound.

It was the door to my apartment. Someone was jiggling the lock. Knowing Ying, I felt sure that the lock he had put on my front door had been purchased at the nearest dollar store. My heart raced. I felt the blood rushing to my face.

I flipped on a light switch and screamed from my bedroom, "Who is it? I have a gun!"

What a stupid thing to say! I'm threatening a potential murderer. I turned on a light. They can see me but I still can't see them. What on God's green earth was I thinking? I looked around the room. Screwed, so screwed. The door was still rattling. Someone was desperate to get in.

Bang! Bang! Bang! The doorknob was being smashed with something. This was it. They were coming in regardless. I wasn't going out without a fight.

I had some stuff from the flea market in my room, one of which was a toy cowboy gun that maybe could pass for a real gun in bad light. I kept the gun at my side hoping that whoever might see it would think that I was armed and might decide to walk away without a fight. As I crept out of my bedroom into the dark kitchen area, I could see a tall figure of a man through the window. I couldn't make out his face. There used to be a single lightbulb that would stay on at night to give the upstairs porch some light, but that bulb had burned out some time ago. Ying never replaced it.

The only shining light was the light from my bedroom, coming from behind me. This was dangerous. The person on the other side of that door could see my silhouette, could pinpoint exactly where I was, but I couldn't make him out too well. I was terrified. My cell phone was lying on a small table in my kitchen. I grabbed it and dialed 9-1-1. The crazy person on the other side of the door kept trying to force the doorknob.

"I'm in my kitchen. There's a man trying to break into my house. I'm terrified," I whispered to the 9-1-1 operator. Too frightened to scream, but then again screaming could be the worst thing I could do. The 9-1-1 operator was calm and just told me to stay on the line and not to hang up.

Finally the intruder was successful. Slowly the door to my apartment opened.

Now was the time to scream.

"Don't come any further or else I'll shoot!" I yelled with the hope of waking up the neighborhood. For only a millisecond, it seemed the footsteps stopped. As the door cracked open, I saw a large dark figure. This was it. I was going to die.

Sirens wailed in the background. This was the beauty of living in downtown Freehold – I wasn't very far away from the police station. The dark figure turned and ran. The next sounds I heard were footsteps rapidly going down the staircase. A car door opened. An engine roared, and the would-be burglar vanished into midnight.

A Crown Vic and two squad cars pulled in shortly after. Bill Baines lead the charge. He flew up the stairs, and I could not have been happier to see him. As expected he had choice words for me.

"*Now* what did you do?"

"Nothing! I'm really getting a little bit sick and tired of all this! First I'm shot at, then someone tries to break into my apartment!" I folded my arms. "What are you going to do about it? This is a Freehold matter. What are *you* doing here?"

"Police business and none of yours." With that ever-daring edge in his voice, he said, "Someone call in a burglar." He removed the toy gun from my hand, pulled the trigger and a limp stream of water trickled out. Baines looked at the gun with disdain as he threw it on a nearby table. "As usual, you had things well in hand."

"Any idea who wants to kill me?"

"No. But you can't stay here tonight."

"Where can I go?"

"Look, I can call our Crime Victims Unit. They can probably get you a place to sleep tonight."

"Sorry. I'm not staying in a welfare hotel. My sister has little kids. She can't take the stress."

He sighed. "Or."

"Or what?"

"I have an extra bedroom where my daughter sleeps when she visits on the weekends. If you don't mind being surrounded by pink ponies and unicorns, you can stay there tonight. But you really can't tell anybody about this."

I just looked at him. "You want me to sleep in your house?"

He folded his arms defiantly, making his biceps appear larger than they were. "I said my house, not my bed."

"Listen, Baines, your bed was not even a remote consideration."

"Honey, don't get your panties in a bunch. You're not my type."

I folded my arms. "What type? Smart? Intelligent?"

He rolled his eyes. "You talk too much. My place or nothing. I don't have all night."

Reality check. I had no options. It was two o'clock in the morning. I couldn't do it to Karrie at this hour, and I couldn't call my sister, so I reluctantly agreed.

"Okay."

"Get in your car and follow me. I am having someone watch this place tonight." He leaned down and whispered, "Remember, let's keep this between us."

I nodded and looked up at him. "Unicorns, eh?"

"Big ones." He smiled. "Grab some clothes and let's go."

CHAPTER 8

Baines lived on the outer edges of Freehold Borough. He pulled in front of a small Cape Cod and parked on the street. He gestured for me to park in his driveway. I felt nervous. I thought this was a nice thing for him to do, I just hoped he didn't expect any "reward" for his good deed.

His home was very neat and clean, but it clearly lacked a woman's touch. In fact, other than pictures of his daughter on the wall, the place was almost stark. Since I was a guest, I didn't feel too comfortable prying into the man's personal life.

He reached into the refrigerator and pulled out a bottle of Guinness. "Would you like?" he asked.

"No thanks. I'm kind of beat. I think I'd just like to go to bed."

"Go down the hall to the left. Lily's room is the first door to your right."

"Okay. Thanks." I paused, deciding whether to tell Baines what Karrie had learned about the artwork we found at Freddie's house. I decided yes. "Listen, I know it's late, but I have to tell you something."

Once again he folded his arms. "No, I am not going to have sex with you tonight."

I was exasperated. "Would you please stop with the sex stuff?"

He gave me this boyish grin that almost broke my heart. "I'm sorry. I'll be serious. What's up?"

"Karrie researched some of the art that we removed from Freddie's house and—"

"You're kidding me, right? I tell you to stay away from that place, so you take stuff from it? Someone nearly blew your head off. You think removing things from the property is a good idea?"

"I didn't take the art. It's at Karrie's house."

"Talk."

I took a deep breath and pulled up a kitchen chair. "I don't know where to start. One of the pictures was stolen from England sometime in the 1990s. She has a Picasso sketchbook that was stolen over twenty years ago. She's got some other kind of art that looks like it's from the 1940s maybe. That stuff has been missing for over twenty years. How it got to Freddie's house, I'll never know. But certainly it's a good enough reason to kill somebody."

Baines looked thoughtful. I saw that the expression on his face was both one of concern and curiosity. I could see that he wasn't sure what to think, but he was thinking.

"Look, several years ago I worked an art case with the FBI. Here's the thing. It's not easy to move stolen art because it isn't a one-person job. It's usually a ring. You got the thief, you got the rogue expert who has to authenticate it, and then you got the black market seller who has to find the black market buyer. But the problem with the stuff that you're talking about is that it's just too hot. You can't simply dump a Picasso sketchbook on a place like Blake and Faraday's or Sotheby's and expect them not to have questions. There's something called provenance. Pieces of art general have a trail of ownership."

"Okay. I get it. That's sort of like the antique stuff I deal with. I mean, I've looked at pieces of porcelain and silver that have been in people's families for years – it was their aunt's or their grandmother's – is that what you mean? Antiques that come with a history?"

"Sort of, yeah. That's it. Fine art is well catalogued by art experts. And then there are these international societies that follow stolen art."

"What are you trying to tell me?"

"I guess what I'm trying to say is that Freddie could not have been working alone. This is way too complicated." He looked over at the wall clock. "And it's way too late for me. I'm on duty starting at seven a.m. Thanks to you, I'll get about five hours' sleep."

I raised an eyebrow and gave him a snarky look. "Sorry. Didn't mean to have someone break into my house in the middle of the night."

"It's fine. Just go to bed."

****

I woke up the next morning in Pink World.

Baines' daughter was serious about pink. The walls were hot pink with a bleached white molding. The ceiling was textured, a pale pinkish tone made with pieces of mother-of-pearl shells that sparkled when rays of morning sunlight bounced off them. Unicorns were everywhere, dangling from the ceiling and standing on the shelves. I was sleeping under a comforter with a laughing unicorn on it. Her room was a pink unicorn fantasy, except for the one lone Barbie doll I'd sold to Baines. She balanced precariously on a shelf next to a water globe with a unicorn and a wizard inside of it.

I got up from the twin bed, and my foot slipped on a small rug, which resulted in me doing a face-plant on a hardwood floor. What a way to start the morning!

Leaving pink unicorn land behind, I headed for the kitchen to forage for breakfast. There was a clean empty coffee cup on the table, a fresh pot of drip coffee, and a small bowl of freshly-cut fruit: melons, strawberries, watermelons, and blueberries. Way too healthy. I went on a hunt for Toaster Strudels. I should've been grateful. At least someone cared about my ever-expanding figure. I poured myself a cup of coffee and sat down to think about what my next move would be. It was at that moment I realized that I had no game plan.

My sister had enough stress raising three children all by herself. I really couldn't involve her in this. It's not that Angela wouldn't help, but my life had become way too complicated at this point. And if a homicidal maniac was chasing me, I didn't want to put small children in the danger zone.

So that left me one option, my only option – my partner in crime, Karrie.

She was tough. I would stay with Karrie until the heat died down, and then move back into my apartment over the Golden Lychee. This would give Ying time to change the locks and perhaps even install a real deadbolt lock. You can't live in fear, but right now

I was, quite candidly, terrified. I just didn't want to be alone, but on the other hand I couldn't stay at Baines' place, even though I felt quite safe there. I gathered my things, called work and told them I would be late, then called Karrie and told her to meet me back at my place after work.

****

Karrie and I arrived at the same time. As we climbed the stairs up to my apartment, we saw a man from Freehold Lock drilling and putting in a new heavy door lock.

"Hi. I guess you have a new key for me."

"No," he stated. "I have a new key for the landlord. I'll give the key to him and he can give it to you."

"I'm right here, and since I live here, you can give it to me."

Finishing his work, he looked up and said one word. "No." Then walked away.

But it seemed that fortune had, in an unusual turn of events, smiled upon me that morning. Ying had just arrived at the restaurant. He came up the stairs and took the new key from the locksmith. He looked over at me and smiled.

"Rox-see, I have new key for you. This is good lock. You can't pick this one."

I looked over at Karrie. She seemed unimpressed by Ying's suggestion of a pick-proof lock. As usual, she couldn't restrain herself from commenting.

"What good is a deadbolt if the poor girl has a door made of cardboard?"

Ying winced. He looked as though someone had slapped him in the face with a glove and challenged him to a duel. He turned to Karrie and pointed a finger.

"Mad-dam, I have you know that that door is solid, like Fort Knox."

To make his point, he went down the stairs, ran back up, and kicked the front door to my apartment with his foot. Upon receiving the blow, the rotting wood around the doorframe collapsed. The entire door, complete with its new deadbolt, fell inside my apartment. I stared at the gaping hole that was once the door.

Ying turned various shades of red. "I call carpenter this afternoon. We get you new door, new lock. I make you safe Rox-see, don't you worry." With that he went back downstairs to the Golden Lychee, muttering to himself in Chinese.

"This is just great. Thank God you'll be staying at my house. Why don't we start moving things that have value so that if anyone comes back they'll be stealing stuff that isn't worth anything?"

"Gee, in that case they can take the whole place. I feel like my whole life is worth about, I don't know, let's see what's in my jeans pocket." I pulled out $2.85. "This is about what my life is worth right now."

Karrie and I went back into my apartment and grabbed clothing. Most of the valuable things I sold were already packed in the SUV and ready to be stored. Ying promised to have the carpenters there in the afternoon to repair the door, but since I didn't know who was going in and out, I packed up anything that I thought would have any value anyway. Off to Karrie's house.

The place was pristine, and there was always plenty to eat. And it was like living in a Victorian museum, with Victoriana and contemporary pieces blending together in a home that probably belonged in Architectural Digest. She was such a good friend to do this for me. I mean, if you think about it, who wants to take in somebody who's being chased by a killer?

We sat down to dinner and plotted our next move with Freddie's estate and the flea market. I figured if I was going to have to defend myself in a lawsuit against Jule Mustergrave, I pretty much had to come up with some money to mount a defense.

My defense was really a very simple one. Mustergrave and her sister were not only not named in the will, but they were specifically excluded from it – that's not just my defense, it's also the law. I also didn't think it made much of a difference whether she'd had dinner with Pynchard or not.

The firm was supposed to be protecting me. She shouldn't be able to retain the same law firm that was defending me – there was that little thing called conflict of interest. But I guess where there was money concerned, ethical obligations didn't really matter. Money is power with certain people, the haves versus the have-nots.

I was on the have nots side of the fence, but that didn't mean that I was going to let myself be pushed around.

CHAPTER 9

It was a sweltering hot Thursday night in June. A call had come in. There was an interesting estate in Rumson that we needed to look at. In the estate business, when opportunity strikes, you move quickly. The saying in this business is: "You die, we buy."

Longer daylight hours gave Karrie and me the opportunity to go out after work and hunt on outdoor estates.

Today was lucky. One of Karrie's former clients had given us a referral to her brother in Rumson. This was very exciting because many millionaires lived along the Navesink River, and they had lots of antiques to sell. Karrie and I had high hopes for this estate; at least it would keep my mind off being shot at by some homicidal maniac who wanted his art back.

We pulled onto Oak Street, and I glanced at Karrie. "Toto, I don't think we're in Kansas anymore."

"You're right," she said with an eager smile. "We're in the Emerald City."

We drove past mansion after mansion along the Navesink River. Manicured lawns, sculptured bushes, old Victorians, and stately homes whose asking price probably started at a million dollars. We looked for 20 Oak Street, cheerfully trying to figure out which mansion held tonight's booty. As only luck would have it, we found it at the end of the block.

It was another eyesore. Among the jeweled mansions with their ocean views, we found the only sea shack that any self-respecting seagull would have avoided flying over.

Our mouths dropped open at the sight of a small, rundown Mid-Century ranch with waist-high weeds and a shopping cart on the front lawn. Somewhere among the weeds, somebody had carved a path to the back of the house, probably out of necessity because the front door was barricaded by another shopping cart and a truck tire. Trekking through the overgrowth to the back of the house was the only way in.

"Do we want to go in?" I asked, praying she'd say no. "I can pass on this one."

"Nonsense. I heard he has Tiffany silver. May be worth looking at."

The back screen door was merely an empty frame, and we were greeted by a nervous, sweaty little man whose legs moved in a tight trot, the kind a first grader does when he has to go to the bathroom. He cheerfully announced that he was unemployed and was looking to sell as many things as possible as quickly as he could.

I couldn't help but think this man needed some serious medication. I wondered if Karrie and I should be alone with him. We entered the house and the stench was enough to kill a horse. The aroma was a mixture of age, dirt, and a perhaps a litter box? Against my better judgment I asked, "Oh, you have any pets?"

"Mother had a cat, Hans, but Hans died about a year ago, and I can't get her to part with any of his things, including his litter box."

"I see."

Poor old Hans probably killed himself to get out of here, I thought.

Looking over at a wreck of an old couch, I saw what looked like a layer of cashmere all over it. Then I realized that his mother really *didn't* part with anything, including Hans's cat hair. The little man continued chattering.

"My name is Kevin. I have this really nice piano I'd like to sell, and I have the silver over here." Karrie gave me a look. I knew the routine.

"Roxie, take a look at that lovely piano, and I'll start looking at the silverware."

Suddenly a funny thing happened. I felt an itch, first one, then two itches, then three until I found myself scratching my legs like a mad woman. I noticed Kevin just kept on trotting in place, talking about the piano and how his mother was a concert pianist. I tried to look at the piano, but I was too busy slapping my legs and doing the scratch dance. I looked over at Karrie, who seemed to be swatting herself nonchalantly. Little invisible critters were taking chunks out of my leg, and I couldn't see where they were coming from. I was being bombarded by some tiny little thing with the bite of a pit bull!

Karrie gathered all the silver in one place. "Roxie, it's a bit too warm in here, dear, I'll just see you outside."

"Fine with me," I said as I swatted my leg for the eightieth time. I looked at the silver and gave it a once-over. "I'll give you a hundred for the lot."

"Okay. But what about the piano? That's worth a lot of money. Let me show you the insides of it."

When he opened up the piano, the biting got worse. Then it finally dawned on me.

Fleas!

This house was full of fleas. I threw the hundred dollars at him, grabbed the silver, and ran out the front door. No estate was worth flea bites. Karrie was already sitting in the car.

"Why didn't you tell me the place was a flea hive?"

"Well I certainly wasn't going to say anything to embarrass that poor little crazy man. Besides, I knew you could handle it. After all, someone tried to kill you, what's a couple of flea bites?" She batted her big blue eyes as she glanced down at her wristwatch. "Time for dinner."

"Yeah, let's hope I didn't drag any unexpected dinner guests along for the ride."

****

After fumigating my body the night before, I went to work at the firm, hoping there wouldn't be an endless day of interrogatories, calls to the court to confirm trial dates for the attorneys, and proof-reading Mac's letters with niggling little grammatical mistakes. The air conditioning was broken in the office, so I was wearing a dress with short sleeves, hoping no one would notice the little red and white marks on my arms as a result of being an appetizer for bunch of fleas.

Mac came over looking for his white shirt, which I'd picked up from the dry cleaner. He was in his usual state of cheerfulness, but his face had a particular exuberance that was frightening. I did know if it was good or bad.

"Hey, Mac, good morning, sir, what's the good word?"

His apple dumpling cheeks were quite rosy as he looked curiously at the flea bites on my arms. "What's with the arms? Measles?"

"No. Don't want to talk about it. Let's just say it's an allergy."

"Well, I have good news for you. And more importantly, I have good news for me."

"Let's start with the good news for you."

"I have a date."

"Do tell. Where did you meet? Online?"

"Yes, a new site called find-me-someone-dot-com."

"Find-me-someone? Sounds like an online site for fugitive retrieval program for parolees."

"Yes, I thought so at first, too. But the pickings, shall I say, were more appropriate for a man of my age. The available ladies weren't eighteen years old or in eighth grade with a third grade reading level. Some of the sites for fifty-plusses had women extracted from the basement of the Great Pyramids of Giza, Roxie. Mummified ladies looking for me to take them on that last thrill ride before the graveyard."

I tried not to laugh. Mac, for all his idiosyncrasies, was a kind and decent soul. He deserved happiness, especially since he'd been taking care of his mother forever after his father died. Mac was a little odd, but he was honest and sincere, and like they say, "There is a shoe for every foot". Glad he found someone in his size.

"So what's my news?"

Mac bent down and spoke in a whisper. "I just thought you'd like to know that our boss referred the Mustergrave matter to another firm. There's a definite conflict of interest. Although I don't understand why Pynchard would have even considered taking it here."

"I never understood why Pynchard ever did anything. And I don't want to find out why."

Mac smiled. "Well, I guess it is the best thing. That Jule Mustergrave seemed quite aggressive. I think she will fight you for that gentleman's estate."

"Have at me. I have nothing to lose. Do you know when that video tape of Freddie's will came into the firm?"

I noted that suddenly Mac's face went a little strange. It seemed that he didn't want to tell me something, but I wasn't going to let him get away with that. So I just came out and asked him.

"You look a little nervous."

"Er, um, the-the videotaped will from Mr. Grant came in about a week before he was murdered. He mailed it to us."

"The week before he was killed, he sent it in. But what was the date that it was actually made? I mean, when was it filmed?"

"If I recall from the film, he dated it April 1, April Fools' Day."

"Wow. Looks like the April Fools' joke was on him. I bet he knew something."

"Like what?"

"Like maybe someone was going to kill him." I felt the blood rising in my face. Too much to think about right now. "Listen, Mac, I have to edit some of your letters, and I have a ton of discovery on this tort case, so I better get back to work. But thanks for telling me that the firm is not taking Mustergrave's litigation."

"I am truly surprised that Mr. Blackwood would have even considered taking this matter after telling everybody our firm is representing you. But I'm afraid that you still have to deal with Jule Mustergrave's wrath." With that, he returned to his office.

That morning I focused on reviewing files, answering interrogatories, and setting up witness interviews. I would be going home to a brand new door and to my crummy, but hopefully safer, apartment. Iceman had spoken to the Freehold Police, and they promised him that they would be doing regular drive-bys past the Golden Lychee.

That was funny because I didn't think that I was important. But I guess since I was the closest thing to a homicide witness, I had some juice. I just hoped that no one would try to "juice" me in the process. Just as I was working on a file, the phone rang. The call had originally come into Old Rainey's office, then Eva Lee sent the call over to my desk.

"Hi, sweetie, it's that good-looking detective on the phone for you," she called over to me.

"Oh boy."

I took a deep breath before I picked up the phone. There was something about his deep, rich baritone – it just kind of melted me from the inside out, even when he was being snarky. He was a purposeful man. There was no reason he would be calling me unless, of course, he wanted something, and it probably wasn't a date.

"Hello, Detective Baines. What can I do for you?"

"How about lunch?"

"What's the catch?"

"Don't get ahead of yourself, Sanchez. This is strictly business. By the way, anyone try to shoot you, blow you up, or burn your house down lately?"

I didn't appreciate sarcasm. "No, I'm happy to say all seems to be eerily peaceful. But I don't know how long that's going to last."

"Here's the deal. Look for a trooper car outside of your office. My buddy, Detective Pete Carsen, is going to pick you up. Will your boss be annoyed if you're a little bit late back to work?"

Now that was a funny question. There were days when I could've taken a two hour lunch, taken in a three hour movie, had my nails done, and no one would've been the wiser. Then when Mr. Blackwood felt the crunch of too few clients coming into the firm, all of a sudden I'd be told I needed to take a half hour lunch and be back on time. It was all about money and time. When there was money, there was always time.

"Everyone but my friend, Mac, is out of the office. If I'm a few minutes late coming back from lunch, I can explain that I had to assist a state trooper with a homicide investigation. He'll understand. I hope."

"Good. I don't think this will take long. Hamilton isn't too far away."

"Hamilton? That's nearly an hour from here!"

"Hang up the phone. Carsen's outside. Bye."

As I hung up the phone, I had lustful thoughts about Iceman's blue eyes until I shook my head back into the moment. From my window, I saw an unmarked Crown Vic and a plainclothesman standing next to the car. I grabbed my purse and ran out the door.

Pete Carsen, I thought. *This should be interesting.*

Compared to Iceman's six-two frame, Carsen looked like he came up to Baines' kneecap. He was bullish looking, with a cherubic face and short-cropped blond hair. I envisioned if he had let his hair grow in its natural state, it would be short and curly. This was my escort: one of Raphael's Sistine Chapel cherubs with a handlebar moustache and chest hair.

"You Roxie?"

"That would be me."

He opened the front passenger door and I got in for what would be the ride of my life. Speed terrifies me, and in a matter of seconds the odometer hit seventy-five. I started hyperventilating. Carsen and I flew down Interstate 195 at breakneck speed. Whatever breakfast still lingered in my stomach churned itself into butter. Carsen must have seen the look on my face and started to chatter.

"How long you known Baines?"

"Since I found a dead guy in a van." The odometer inched up to eighty five. "Do you think you could slow down a bit? I'd like to remain with the living for a few more years."

"Aw, don't worry, hon." He dropped down to seventy-five. "I make you nervous? You know I drive for a living, right?"

"What? A taxi in Manhattan?"

He laughed. "No, but I'll dial it down for ya." When the trees lining Interstate 195 stopped looking like elongated green blurs, I knew we were finally doing about fifty-five.

"Thanks. Where is this place?"

"State Police Forensic Lab. That's where we took the murder weapon that killed your vendor friend."

"I see."

"Sad about that poor old bastard. Who'd he ever hurt, right? I knew him from Columbia Meadows. Bought some tools off him once. They turned out to be crap, but it was okay. I only lost five bucks."

"Ever buy any artwork off Freddie?"

"Not into art, really. Didn't think he actually sold that kind of stuff. Why, was he an *artiste?*"

I thought about the Picasso sketchbook. "No, I just think he knew one or two artists, that's all. Did you ever see him selling any artwork?"

"You playing detective now?" he laughed.

"No. Just wondering."

When we arrived at the Hamilton facility, I breathed a sigh of relief as I heard the Crown Vic's gear shoved into park. The place was a huge, impressive facility, and I could see where a lot of sophisticated police investigations could go on in this place. Carsen and I cleared security and began walking the long stretch down the hallway. Against a white background I saw Iceman leaning against the wall with his arms folded. I actually saw a half smile on his face. It was a sexy smile, but it still made me feel like I was the prey and he was the hunter.

I hated to admit my own weakness, but this guy made me nervous. It was that annoying, sickening, butterfly-in-the-stomach schoolgirl nervousness. I hated that. The only thing I hated more was the fact he made me feel that way.

I think the last time I had a case of butterflies in the stomach was over my seventh grade crush, Ricky Willis. Ricky had this wonderful shock of dark hair, incredibly sensual green eyes, and a pair of braces in his mouth that ran ear-to-ear. Ricky told me that he planned to be a doctor someday. A man with a touch of brain...*sigh*. In seventh grade, he would smile at me, metal mouth and all, and I would just melt. I ran into his mother several years ago, and she showed me a picture of Ricky, happily stating that he was still available.

But oh, how the mighty had fallen. The picture revealed a fat, bald guy with a beer gut who worked for J.R. Landscaping. Like they say, you can never go home.

We continued down the hallway. As we grew closer, Carsen yelled to Iceman. "Package delivered. I'm outta here."

"Thanks, bro. See you tomorrow." Iceman turned to give me his full attention. "Nice to see you, Sanchez."

"Baines." *Here I go again*, I thought.

"Oh, I forgot. Ms. Sanchez."

"Is this going to take long? I have to get back to work."

"I called your boss while Pete was on his way here. Rainey Blackwood told me, 'When you get her back, you get her back.'"

"I didn't know you had so much power."

He snickered. "I don't. Follow me."

He led me down the hall to a small room off the main corridor and opened the door with a key. Inside I saw a plastic bag containing a carved red-handled knife. A chill came over me. That must've been the knife I saw sticking out of Freddie that fateful Saturday morning in Columbia Meadows. My stomach started to bunch up.

"Our lab has already examined the knife. Freddie's blood was all over it, but we couldn't lift a single fingerprint." He handed me the knife in the plastic bag.

"You have any Pepto-Bismol? I could really use some right now."

Iceman didn't flinch, but his eyes softened somewhat when he looked at me. "Stay with me on this for a minute. That knife handle's some kind of an antique, right?"

The handle was a heavy opaque, carved cherry red plastic. From what I could see, the blade of the knife was embedded in the molded plastic in the shape of a stag's horn. "The knife handle looks like Bakelite to me."

"Educate me. What's Bakelite?"

"It's an early plastic that was very popular in the jewelry industry back in the 1940s but it was also used in cars and radios. This knife handle looks like Bakelite, but you'd have to test it. Can I put this down now?" I wanted to be anywhere in the world except in the room with the murder weapon.

"How do you test for Bakelite?"

"You can use something called Simichrome or Formula 409 cleaner. Put some on a cotton ball and touch it to the knife handle. If it flashes yellow, you have Bakelite. If not, you have some other kind a plastic."

He nodded and then picked up the telephone. He told whoever was on the phone to get down here with some Formula 409. He turned to me.

"This was helpful. Anything else?"

"I already told you everything I know. But there is something else. From the look of this knife, it was probably part of a set. I'm guessing that this was a carving set. Which means that somewhere out there is its mate. Can I ask you a question?" I plopped down in a near by chair.

"Go."

"You don't have any suspects, do you? I mean, let's face it, you wouldn't be asking me for help if you had this whole thing wrapped up like a burrito, right?"

The look on his face became one of complete disgust. But this time I didn't think the disgust had anything to do with me for a change. He was frustrated and I sensed it.

"I can't get into the details of the investigation, Sanchez, but let's just say this. Nobody liked this guy, and nobody cared about him. The only people who seem to care even remotely about him right about now are his two sisters. They appear to be after the money. And they seem to think you killed him."

I felt my blood pressure going up. "I wouldn't be surprised if his sisters killed him. He hated them. He left them ten cents to split between the two of them. After meeting Jule Mustergrave, I understand why he left her a nickel. I would have left her a penny."

A strange smile came across Iceman's face.

"I don't like that look you're giving me," I said. "I hope you don't think I had anything to do with this guy's death." I rose out of my chair.

There it was again. That sexy half smile that tugged at my heartstrings. It was unfair. This guy was such a bad boy, and I was starting to have a taste for him.

"Sanchez, you're too much of a klutz to kill anyone. If you killed anyone, you would probably do something stupid like blow yourself up in the process."

"Thanks a lot. What about the art?"

"What about it?"

"Could he have been killed because of the art?"

"Could be. Don't know. What's the status of your probate case?"

"I'm waiting to be sued by Freddie's sisters. Karrie is storing some of the art we picked up at her house. We were thinking of contacting the FBI. Like I told you, the art is stolen."

With a pensive look, Iceman asked, "Sanchez, what's some flea market bum doing with stolen art?"

"I take umbrage to that last statement. We flea market vendors are not 'bums.' And apparently Freddie came from, as his nasty sister reminded me, a very old family. Somebody in Freddie's family has lots of this." Rubbing my thumb and forefingers together, I made the universal sign for money. "Maybe the art was in his family. But I don't know."

"Well, I heard that he had a huge fight with Eddie Collins, Columbia Meadows's owner, over the price of his rental space. Happened about three weeks ago. But Eddie had an alibi the morning of the murder. He was in Miami. You know, everybody seems to hate Freddie."

"That's a fair statement. My friend Karrie hates him because he broke some kind of Native American basket of hers. Fell into her table and smashed it when he was three sheets to the wind, which from all accounts was a fairly regular occurrence. But Karrie was with me most morning."

"Are you telling me that if I am looking for a murder suspect, I better take a number."

I shrugged. "Uh, yes?"

CHAPTER 10

Karrie and I wanted to check out another "asset" of Freddie's estate, the *Bearded Lady*. Having seen the likes of Freddie's house, I could only imagine what his boat looked like. As I recalled from the warm and fuzzy meeting I had with my bosses, Iceman, and Mr. Queecy, the boat was supposed to be a dilly. I don't know if I could stand inheriting any more "dillies" from Freddie. Freddie's legacy was killing me slowly, steadily, daily in incremental bits, not unlike arsenic poisoning.

Mr. Queecy had given me the slip number at the Parsells Marina where the boat had been docked. Apparently before Freddie kicked the bucket, he paid all the marina fees for the entire summer of the current season, plus the upcoming winter. I was happy about this because at least I didn't have to pay out anything. However, my friend Karrie felt distinctly different.

I don't know what I'd do without Karrie. I always enlisted her. If I were Lucy Ricardo, she was my Ethel Mertz. Unfortunately, we had a dead "Fred Mertz" on our hands, and my "Ethel" seemed pretty happy about it. She was very concerned about the whole estate thing and was waiting for some dirty trick by Freddie at the end of the probate period. Personally, I just don't think Freddie was that clever. Karrie felt differently, but she agreed to join me in the search for the infamous *Bearded Lady*.

I picked Karrie up and we headed to Parsells Marina, a small marina located in Point Pleasant, New Jersey. The day was clear, blue, and cloudless, not unlike the day I found dear old dead Fred. There was a nice sea breeze, so Karrie and I weren't roasting in the eighty-six degree heat. But with her wide-brimmed sun hat and SPF 250 sunblock, Karrie was ready for summer.

Time to hunt for a yacht.

After parking the car in the lot at the marina, we looked for the old dockmaster and owner, Jimmy Parsells. At the end of the dock, we saw a white beard, gray hair, and a Greek fisherman's cap on a man in the process of tying a boat to the dock. My best guess told me that this salty seaman was Jimmy Parsells. As we approached, he stopped what he was doing and lit a skinny cigar in complete defiance of all the very obvious "No Smoking" signs posted all over the marina.

"Beautiful ladies so early in the morning? To what do I owe this pleasure?" He looked at Karrie. "Say, haven't we met? Aren't you Bill Langston's ex-wife?"

"No, I'm Bill Langston's mother!" she snapped. "And you are?"

"The owner of this fine establishment." He offered a weather-beaten hand. "Jimmy Parsells. What can I do you for?"

I looked at Karrie. This couldn't be good. She was giving Jimmy the old stink eye, and then she turned to me. The unspoken message was: talk fast.

"Mr. Parsells, I am, uh…"

"Call me Jimmy, please."

"I'm looking for a boat. It belonged to a friend of mine who recently died. I understand that I inherited it. It's a yacht called the *Bearded Lady*."

At first Jimmy snickered a bit. Then he chuckled. Suddenly the old man burst out laughing so hard, I thought he was going to wet his pants. "Yeah, I read that Freddie took the dirt nap in the newspaper. Nice man. Too bad. Dead like a doornail. I'll show you where the yacht is." He snickered. "Come with me."

Yacht, I thought. *How bad could it be?* A few seconds later, I was truly sorry I had asked.

We walked past several fifty-foot cabin cruisers. These boats were fiberglass mansions that happened to float across water. After we moved past several more luxury yachts, Jimmy pointed to a twenty-six foot gray boat with peeling paint and a small wheelhouse. It was in terrible shape, and I was surprised to see that it wasn't *under* the water instead of on top of it. Amidst the peeling paint, there was a portrait of a fat mermaid with clam shells for a bra, and a long red beard that had gold fish tangles inside of it.

I wanted to pour gasoline all over this demented barge, then give it a nice Viking funeral at sea. Karrie must've seen the look on my face because she put a sympathetic hand on my shoulder. She must've noticed that my eyes were welling up. Freddie screwed me again.

"Listen," Karrie whispered, "my ex knows Jimmy pretty well. I'll make a phone call to him and he'll help us dump the boat. Probably has scrap value. But I think we should go inside and take a look around."

"Karrie, you don't think he has artwork stored on this yacht? How can he call this a yacht? It's a bathtub with a motor, a floating slum."

"Yes dear, but it's a twenty-six foot bathtub, which puts it in the yacht category." She turned to Jimmy and waved the set of keys that belong to the *Bearded Lady*. "Jimmy, we'd like to board please, and the boat drifted out from the dock a little bit. Can you bring her back in so that this young lady and I can board?"

"Sure thing, missy." Jimmy grabbed a rope that anchored the yacht and pulled the *Bearded Lady* next to the dock. He placed a rickety gang plank in a break in the railing and jumped on board. Once on the boat Jimmy extended a hand and helped Karrie and me aboard. I looked at Karrie. She was wearing those pristine white slacks again.

"You amaze me. How do you keep those things so white?"

"Better question," She pointed to my capris that had a big black greasy-looking mark at the knee. "How did you manage to find dirt so quickly?"

I looked at the grease spot. "Wow. Didn't see that one." We both laughed. "Just a dirt magnet, I guess."

"Let's get on with this, shall we? Who knows what treasures lurk in this oversized rowboat?"

"Now that made me feel so much better," I said sarcastically. "I don't know if I can take any more of these surprises."

Karrie made a beeline to the tiny wheelhouse that stuck out of the top of the *Bearded Lady*, and I followed close behind. Upon entering, we saw several loose folders next to the captain's wheel. When I moved them, I also noticed a small thumb drive lying underneath the folders. I thought it was odd, because Fred didn't exactly strike me as being computer literate. I handed Karrie the folders and shoved the thumb drive into my purse.

There were some tiny cabinets below deck. Jimmy came down, popped his head into the wheelhouse, and said, "Ladies, you're welcome to take a run down there, but I don't see nothing of any value. Just some old junk."

"Junk?" I looked at Karrie. She looked at me. Simultaneously we both said, "Let's look."

The tiny cabin was dark. Using my cell phone as a flashlight, we went down a small set of steps leading to the chum bucket's sleeping quarters. I saw a couple of slips where some unfortunate sailor may have slept. I heard the discomforting splish-splash of a marine toilet in the middle of the hull. On one of the slips I noticed some metallic-looking items: two lanterns, a ship's bell, and something that looked like a small woman's powder compact. When I picked up the compact, the lid popped open. It was an old compass. All of these items had a lot of age to them. Freddie was on to something here. I handed Karrie the bell and placed the compass in my purse as we each grabbed a lantern.

I was sure that if Freddie were alive, he would be taking these things to the market or putting them up on eBay. Now they were mine, and I would do the same thing once I had cleared the estate. In appreciation of Karrie's help, I offered her one of the lanterns. It was the least I could do for dragging her on my latest escapade.

Once we were topside again, we ran into Jimmy. We asked him if there were any other parts of the boat that we hadn't seen. He said no. He also said something interesting: Apparently, Karrie and I were not the first ones to explore the *Bearded Lady* after Freddie's death.

"Yeah, some people came on the boat when I wasn't here. Found this out from one of the young guys hanging around the dock. I yelled at them, you know. I says to them, I says, 'Why are you letting people into the marina when you don't know who they are?'"

"Stupid question, Jimmy. How did you who know *I* was?"

"Freddie mentioned to me, you know, we was pretty good friends, me and Freddie, we used to go out and check out the stars together. June first we would always head out in the *Bearded Lady* here, sit out on the ocean, look at Antares, and have a couple of pops. Freddie considered himself an amateur astronomer, you know."

Karrie rolled her eyes. "Oh a virtual Galileo."

Jimmy continued. "Freddie told me that if anything happened to him, you would be coming out here. But them other guys, they came out here when no one was around to check things out. I wasn't here that day."

"Do you know if they took anything from the boat?" I asked.

"I wasn't here, so I don't know for sure. These young kids told me after the fact. But they should be working here tomorrow, and I'll ask them again. You know how these kids are. They don't pay attention to much around them, too busy with their cell phones and that Facebook stuff."

Karrie looked thoughtful. "I think we've seen enough here today." She looked at her watch. "It's almost twelve-thirty. Way past my lunchtime. Shall we go to the Court Jester for an afternoon cocktail?"

"Why not? I hear Dr. Cosmo calling."

"Dr. Cosmo?"

"Yeah, my ice cold pink lime vodka therapist. When life gets too complicated, there's always Dr. Cosmo."

****

Two cosmos later, a thick, juicy Jester burger with Wisconsin cheddar and French fries burned to my liking had given me the strength to go back to my apartment. Even though I had a nice comfortable buzz from the lunch activities, when I started to open

Freddie's files, I felt nervous all over again, wondering what kind of mess I would find. I made a note to myself to call Mr. Queecy and inform him that while he was busy telling me not to go near the Colts Neck house, somebody apparently knew about Freddie's boat and decided to take liberties with it. Someone was trying to steal from the estate. Not cool.

I kept thinking that my dear friend Mac Ferguson used the right term when he quoted *Alice in Wonderland* saying "curiouser and curiouser." I'm a person who needs organized chaos, so I made a list of what I knew to date about this whole mess.

I met a guy named Freddie at a flea market. I found a guy named Freddie stone cold dead in his van. Freddie owned a house in Colts Neck, which at one time was probably nice. He apparently had some money to buy the house in Colts Neck as well as a crummy boat. How did Freddie make his money? Well, it couldn't have been selling broken screwdrivers. He must have come from money, though at this time, I wasn't sure how much. But certainly it must be enough to make his two sisters fight me for it. What I don't understand is how we came across millions of dollars' worth of stolen art.

The only people who knew about the stolen art in Freddie's possession were Karrie and Iceman. I hadn't mentioned it to anyone at work – to Mr. Queecy, Mr. Blackwood, or Mr. Pynchard. While the law firm where I worked was representing me, I just felt a little paranoid. I knew eventually I would have to tell them about the artwork, but I just wasn't ready for that yet. I was very curious as to what I would find on that thumb drive, so I opened it up on my computer.

I was speechless. Freddie had taken photographs of the paintings that we had figured out were stolen. There were multiple paintings of what look like people interred in some kind of prison camp; I think I had counted about sixteen in total. He had photographed every single page of the Picasso sketchbook, *The White Duck* by Jean-Baptiste Oudry, a *Madonna and Child* painting that had a real medieval look to it, and other artwork. I could only think that he stole all the stuff, knew people might be coming after him, and decided that somehow photographing it all and keeping the list may have protected him. Question: protect him from whom?

Against my better emotional judgment, I picked up the telephone and wondered if I should call Iceman on his cell. I wasn't sure if I should do this, but I felt like I was wearing my poor friend Karrie out. I figured Iceman was law enforcement, and he was used to being worn out by people. I called him.

"Hello?" A little girl's voice answered the phone.

Oh crap. "Hello, may I speak to Detective Baines please?"

I heard the little girl's voice yell "Daddy!" The next thing I knew I heard a rich baritone voice on the other end of the phone.

"Baines?" I asked.

"Sanchez? To what do I own this distinct pleasure? Let me guess, someone tried to kill you again." He laughed.

"No, not today. But I found something interesting. Karrie and I went out to see the *Bearded Lady*."

"I didn't know the Ringling Brothers were in town. Wasn't she in the sideshow?"

I could picture Iceman's full lips bursting out to a very wide smile. "This is serious. Karrie and I went on Freddie's boat down at Parsells Marina. When we boarded the ship, I mean barnacle barge, I grabbed some folders and a thumb drive. I opened up the thumb drive, and I saw photographs of some of the pictures we grabbed from the house."

"You got my attention."

"The thumb drive had on it pictures of the stuff that Karrie found on the Internet that was stolen, the Picasso sketchbook, and *The White Duck*. And then there were pictures – a lot of pictures – of art that looks like it was an interpretation of some kind of a prison in a foreign country."

"But that still doesn't explain how a guy that sells junk came across millions of dollars of stolen art."

"You didn't let me finish. Besides the thumb drive, there were a bunch of folders with papers in them from an outfit called U-STORIT. About six months ago, Freddie paid five hundred dollars for a storage locker from an outfit called U-STORIT. Baines, think like that TV show, *Storage Wars*."

I heard Iceman's sigh on the other of the phone. "Do you mean that place out on Route 9 in Clearwater Township?"

"Yes."

"Very shady joint. One of our task forces did a bunch of buy and busts on their premises about six months ago. It was amazing the amount of cocaine that was being run through a place supposedly renting storage units. We arrested the old owner who's now doing time in Riverfront Prison. Dude was a real squirrel. My understanding is that a new set of his squirrelly relatives bought it."

"Karrie and I will go there tomorrow. We have to start talking to the new owner. I think we need to know who owned this unit before Freddie."

"No! You and I will go out. Leave Karrie out of this. Why do you insist on dragging that poor old lady into all your adventures?"

For half a minute, I thought Iceman may have actually been concerned about my well-being. Apparently not. But I heard the stubbornness in his voice, and since I had spent a lot of time irritating him, I figured I better let this one go. "So what time do you want to go?"

"Will call you at work tomorrow. Listen, my little girl is calling me. Gotta bounce." Iceman hung up.

****

Another uneventful day at work.

I had drafted several transmittal letters for His Royal Majesty King Pynchard the Worst. As usual, Pynchard was in his typical jolly mood. He was not a morning person, hadn't had his coffee yet, and anyone who was in his way was an easy target to be gutter sniped by him. He had filed several motions on a huge construction contract case he had been working on. He made corrections to his work and told me to fix them. I made changes to his document, spell checked it, then returned it to him for one last look before filing. Pynchard changed my corrections back to the way he had written it the first time. When he was done, he screamed at me for not correcting the document properly the first time. And of course, none of the errors had anything to do with him.

This was typical Edward Pynchard. I used to get my feelings really hurt by this, but it was such a regular occurrence, I had become immune to his insults. It was very frustrating, correcting a document then re-correcting it to its original state. It was like shoveling sand against an ocean tide. No matter how hard you worked, no matter what you did, you were simply going nowhere fast.

Eva Lee was wearing a particularly tight fire engine red skirt that day with matching patent leather stiletto heels. Instead of buzzing me, she trotted over, looking excited.

"Hey, Eva, what's up?"

"Detective Hottie left a message for you. He said that he'll pick you up after work to head to the storage place. He asked me to make sure you got the message."

"Thanks, Eva. I got the message." I noticed that she looked at the nasty messages written across the letters I had typed for Pynchard.

"Why is Pynchard so mean, Roxie?"

"Don't mind this stuff, Eva, he does this to me all the time."

She bristled. "Ignore him, sweetie. He's so different from Old Rainey. What a stick in the mud!" With that remark, she trotted back to her desk.

****

Baines said that he would be there at five o'clock. He arrived right on time. We got an unmarked car and sped down Route 9 until we hit Clearwater Township. It was a big, several acre storage unit, used either by people in transit to store furniture while they were moving or to store items that they didn't want to keep on their premises. Either way, anything at U-STORIT was stuff that couldn't be stored in a home.

After we passed through the gates of U-STORIT, there was a tiny office right before the storage units. Baines and I parked the car and went into the office. As we opened the door, a tiny bell smashed against the glass top of the door, making an annoying tinkling sound that woke up the sleeping man behind the desk. He ran his hand through his greasy hair quickly and stood up.

"Can I help you?"

I watched as Baines went into police mode. It was a quiet yet commanding presence. "Yeah, I'd like some information about one of your units."

"You want to rent? If you don't, I don't give out no information about other people's units. People are entitled to their privacy here. They pay for it." He sat down and picked up a newspaper lying open on his desk. He made believe he was reading as he jammed his chubby little hand into a bag of Cheez Doodles. It was the ultimate diss. He held the newspaper in front of his face, pretending to read it so he could ignore us.

Baines looked over and winked at me. I wanted to melt. I watch the way he cocked his head and looked at the greasy little man behind the counter. The lion was sizing up its prey right before he pounced.

"Well sir, it seems like my girlfriend here–"

"Girlfriend?"

Baines gave me a dirty look. "My girlfriend here inherited a storage unit from a friend of hers who was murdered."

Upon hearing the word "murdered," the man dropped the newspaper. "What was murdered? I run a clean operation here. I don't have any dead bodies in storage."

I interjected, "Not what, *who*. My friend Freddie Grant used to own unit 1104. He died a couple weeks ago and I inherited his estate. I understand he bought the contents of an abandoned storage unit from you for five hundred bucks."

"Look, unless you have paperwork, I ain't showing you jack. Maybe I'll just call my lawyer," he stated as he punched in a number on his cell phone.

Before the call went through, Baines reached over the counter, ripped the phone out of his hand and flung it against the wall. He then proceeded to flash his badge. I watched in amazement. The man was a magician.

"You got a name, pal?"

"N-N-ick Pontocurso. I'm the new owner, actually."

"Okay Nick, you bought this place from your sleazebag cousin Ralph Pontocurso, who got busted with a bunch of his little friends last month for running large quantities of coke through this joint. Now you're telling me that you're legit? I doubt it."

"Oh, but I am, I am. I don't want no trouble here. Look, look, I'll tell you what I know. I got all the paperwork right here. Gimme a sec." He put on a pair of reading glasses, walked over to a file cabinet, and started pulling paper. "Okay, Freddie Grant came in here and he bought unit 1104."

"We already know that," I stated. "What I want to know is who owned it before Freddie? Who abandoned the unit?"

"Okay, I got the file right here. It looks like ten months ago somebody named Ernst Steichenhahl came in here and stored his stuff, and this is what it says, folks: 'home furnishings from his summer house in Vienna.' After six months he stopped paying. Now I have a whole bunch of letters here that I personally sent this man, telling him that he needs to pay back rent on the unit or else I put it up for auction as abandoned property. U-STORIT sent him letters by certified and regular mail. Then the mail all came back. Tried to call him by phone and it was disconnected. U-STORIT did everything by the book."

"What was Steichenhahl's address?" Baines asked.

"The letters went to 461 Fifth Avenue in Lake Como, New Jersey. Everything came back from the post office saying that he moved and left no forwarding address. I filed these court papers, so Mr. Steichenhahl's stuff went to auction as abandoned property. I did everything legit, see? Here are the letters from the lawyer's office. Everything we sent to this guy came back." Pontocurso handed me the documents.

Baines looked over at me. "What do you think?"

I looked at the mailings from U-STORIT to Mr. Steichenhahl. "This gentleman is correct. He provided the former owner with all the right notices. We've done this kind of thing at the firm before when we seized property. Can we take a look at the unit? Is there anything left in there?"

"I think Freddie pretty much took everything. But wait—" He reached on the wall and handed me a set of keys. "Go have a look for yourself. It's building G #75, all the way in the back, on the right-hand side. Freddie and I broke the lock once but then Freddie came back and put a new lock on it. Here. Take the keys for the new lock."

Baines smiled at him. "Thank you for your cooperation, Nicky. Much appreciated." He turned to me. "Let's go have a look."

****

Baines and I drove to the far end of the lot and found storage unit 1104. Just as I suspected, it was the dirtiest, dingy little unit in the entire place. I didn't expect any better from Freddie. I'd gotten used to the idea that he was going to be leaving me garbage. I already had a ramshackle house, a crappy boat, and now I owned a crappy storage unit. I took the keys and opened the huge padlock on the door to the unit. It opened like a garage door. It was heavy, and Baines gave me a hand lifting up the door. He stood very close to me, and I felt the pheromones rising, but it was the wrong time to start getting excited about him.

As the door started opening up, a big fat rat came running out the door. I screamed. "That's it! I'm done! I don't want to see anything else in here!" I started heading back to the Crown Vic.

Baines put his hands on my shoulders. "Look, man up. Or in your case, woman up. Put your big girl panties on. You've come too far, and we're starting to make some headway here. Besides," he laughed, "rats don't eat much."

"Thanks. I feel so much better."

A single lightbulb on a thin electrical wire dangled from the ceiling. Immediately Baines started searching for a switch and found it. Clicking the switch, the incandescent bulb lit the entire unit. I took a deep breath.

There was bronze statuary, oil paintings, etchings, and gouaches. The paintings all looked like they had a lot of age to them; in fact, all of the artwork had a lot of age. Baines and I started turning over each piece of art. Every piece had a single brown paper sticker on the back that read: "Sicherges durch den Einsatzstab RR, Stabsfuhrung". The typing looked like it came from an old manual typewriter, the likes of which my mother probably used in high school back in the seventies. I looked over at Baines, who was studying a painting.

"What do you think?"

"Well, this one is signed by Renoir. It's either the real deal or a very nice-looking fake. What was your friend into?"

I just couldn't get across to Baines or anyone else that Pack Rat Freddie and I were not best friends. He was a guy I saw at a flea market once in a while. He wasn't related to me, and I knew nothing about him. If he was a barbed wire collector, I wouldn't have known about it. I couldn't get it through anyone's head, Baines included, that this guy was truly someone I knew nothing about. As I was getting to know more about Freddie, I found it frightening.

He was either running an art fraud ring and that was why he was offed by somebody, or he was selling repros and trying to pass them off as genuine. Selling a fake to the wrong wealthy black market collector could also get you killed. However, no matter who killed Freddie, he was dead, buried, and I got left with a leaky bag of doody.

"Look, I don't know what he was into. I'm not an art expert, you have people in museums for that. Besides, I wonder whatever happened to Mr. Steichenhahl. We know where Freddie got the art. Now the questions is why did Mr. Steichenhahl abandon the art? What happened to him?"

We had been there for nearly an hour. Baines got on the phone and was having a team come down to pick up the paintings. He had the perfect excuse: evidence in a crime. But I had a slightly different idea.

"Baines, let me take one of these paintings to Blake and Faraday's or Sotheby's in New York. Let's see if we can authenticate them."

"Pick one."

"I'll take this one."

Carrying a huge canvas into Manhattan would be a disaster for me. I picked up a kind of interesting eighteen-inch-tall painting of a man wearing a big sombrero on his way to work. I also had one of the prisoner of war paintings at Karrie's house. That would be enough. I would take these two to Blake and Faraday's or Sotheby's. If these were just cheap reproductions, then suffice it to say they were probably all fakes.

As more state police officers arrived, each grabbed a painting and loaded it onto a truck. In a strange way, I felt sorry for these inanimate objects. If they were fakes, they probably had a long voyage from China. If they were genuine pieces of stolen art, then they had been severely mistreated for the past fifty years or so, being improperly stored or secreted away. Either way, now they would be stuffed in an evidence vault in Trenton somewhere, hidden from the world until someone figured out what to do with them.

Nick Pontocurso came running from his office when he saw the other squad cars coming in. He stood before Baines breathlessly, wearing a vintage 1980s black Members Only jacket. I guess he was the last living member.

"Officer, I see a lot of action here. Everything good?"

Baines folded his arms and grinned. "It's all good, Nicky."

"Great, great. I just wanted to make sure there were no drugs on the premises. I run a clean operation here since you locked up cousin Ralphie."

"I'll bet," Baines sneered.

CHAPTER 11

I called Karrie that night to tell her my news, but it was a battle of who could get their words out faster. We wound up talking over each other until I finally said, "Karrie, I give up. You go first – what's your news?"

"Did I ever tell you about my Aunt Violet's son's wife's first cousin, Elliott?"

This was one of those moments when I felt ready to tear my hair out strand by strand. All I could say was, "No, Karrie, you never told me about your Aunt Violet's son's wife's first cousin, Elliott."

"That's funny, I thought I talked about either him or my Aunt Violet."

"You're killing me here. What's your point?"

"Well you see, Elliott works at Blake and Faraday's auction house in New York."

"You mean *the* Blake and Faraday's, right?"

"The very same. As luck would have it, Aunt Violet called her son's wife's first cousin–"

"Elliott," I stated flatly.

"Right. Elliott doesn't handle European art, he's into more Roman antiquities, that sort of thing. But we have an appointment with the curator there who is familiar with European art. And I'm happy to say, I was able to wangle an appointment with a Mr. Archibald Brindles."

****

Karrie and I took the train over to West 21ˢᵗ Street in Manhattan where Blake and Faraday's was located. Upon arriving at our destination, we entered the lobby and stood at their information desk. From the look on the man's face, I probably could have walked into his house, spat on his kitchen floor, and made the same impression. I felt like I was way out of my league. Karrie did not.

"Good afternoon, sir. Mr. Elliott Worth has scheduled an appointment with a Mr. Archibald Brindles and–"

"Dr. Brindles. You have an appointment with *Dr.* Brindles."

"Do you mind? I would like to finish my sentence without interruption. We have an appointment with Dr. Brindles, and we are quite busy as I have an appointment across town to appraise an estate. Time is money, you know. These are important pieces of art in our possession. If Blake and Faraday's isn't interested, I am sure Sotheby's will be."

I looked at the floor. Because if I looked at Karrie, I was going to burst out laughing. After looking at the flea hive in Rumson, Blake and Faraday's was a long way from home and the kind of estates we were used to appraising. Here they sell $400,000 Federal tables. We sold vintage Barbies, Depression glass and costume jewelry.

"Of course Madam. If you're seeing Dr. Brindles, these must be important pieces. Follow me, please."

He directed us to a small room off the main hallway. Inside there was a very large ceiling light, a desk, telephone, and three chairs. Had the decor been just a little more barren, it could've been an interrogation room in a police station. We sat for fifteen of the longest minutes of my life until a door opened and a short, impeccably dressed bald man entered the room. He was all about business.

"Good afternoon, I'm Dr. Brindles. May I see what you have, please?"

"Do I detect a British accent, Dr. Brindles? Oxford, perhaps?"

Karrie tried to work her charm on him, but he was having none of it.

"Cambridge actually. May I see the paintings please?"

I handed him the painting of the guy wearing the sombrero who appeared to be heading off to work with a canvas under his arm. I watched as Dr. Brindles raised an eyebrow, then removed a jeweler's loupe from his breast pocket and carefully examined the painting, looking at it brushstroke by brushstroke. He raised his head and glared at me.

"Is this some kind of a bad joke?"

"Excuse me?"

Dr. Brindles turned the painting over and placed his hands over his lips as though he were suppressing a scream.

"I found it in a storage unit, in a place called U-STORIT in South Jersey. I have no idea who painted it."

"Just bear with me for a minute. I have to call someone." Dr. Brindles rapidly dialed a telephone number and began speaking in a language neither Karrie nor I recognized. I leaned over to her and whispered, "You know, I have the distinct feeling this whole thing's going to blow up in our faces."

"And I have the distinct feeling we should let them have the paintings and run. On my count, out the door. Get up on three. One, two-"

We jumped to our feet. Too late. Karrie and I both stared in amazement. Blocking the doorway was a familiar face. It was the new vendor from the auction, David Williams. And he wasn't smiling.

While Karrie and I sat there with our mouths open, Dr. Brindles made introductions. "Mrs. Langston and Ms. Sanchez, I'd like you to meet Avi Antares, an intelligence agent from Israel currently working with the FBI on a stolen art ring."

I couldn't believe it. *He* was Avi Antares. He was probably the guy who signed the memorial book during Freddie's wake. I guess Freddie's wasn't the only ghost at the wake because I never saw him come in. He was well dressed, and I could still see his muscles bulging beneath the tailored suit. He wasn't as tall as Iceman, but he made up for it in bulk. His hair was smoothed down and in that same ponytail. I also couldn't help but notice the gun he had holstered.

Karrie looked at me as I studied him and, of course, made one of her typical remarks. She leaned over to me and whispered, "This isn't the time to go gaga over the gun-toting man in the expensive suit. He's probably a Mossad agent who is going to kill us and make it look like an accident."

The very serious look faded from Avi's face when he overheard Karrie's remark. His full wide lips parted and gave us a smile. I wondered if that was the smile he gave right before he assassinated somebody.

"Would you or Dr. Brindles mind telling me what kind of painting this is?" One last question before I died.

Avi Antares piped up. "Do you like stories, ladies? If you do, I have a good story for you. Better than the best bedtime store you have ever heard. Would you like a cup of tea?"

Karrie leaned over. "Don't take the tea. He's going to poison us."

David laughed. "Ms. Karrie, I'm standing right here."

Dr. Brindles picked up the telephone and ordered tea for the four of us. Karrie and I were extremely nervous because it was obvious that Avi was not who we thought he was. But then again, who was he? Law enforcement yes, but from the size of his biceps, he *was* the law, and now we were in the middle of a hotbed of illegal activity. I tried to calm my nerves as Avi started to explain.

"You ladies are in no trouble at all. Take a deep breath and relax." He turned his head to look at the door that had begun to open. "Ah, very good, our tea has arrived."

A woman in a delightful old-fashioned maid's outfit pushed in the tea cart, along with a tray of butter cookies. Karrie's eyes bugged. She loved cookies, and she immediately reached for one. I was too nervous to eat, and I was afraid that everything was probably poisoned. Sounds ridiculous, but it was just my genuine paranoia about things lately. As we were being served, Avi began to talk.

"Everyone remembers the history of World War II, yes?"

"I do." Karrie turned to me. "Of course I was only an infant at the time."

"During that time, Nazis led by a man named Alfred Rosenberg began stealing art masterpieces from France, Poland, Germany, and Italy. These masterpieces stolen by the Nazis were catalogued with a particular stamp as part of Einsatzstab Reichsleiter Rosenberg, or ERR."

Karrie interrupted. "Are you telling us that this is stolen Nazi art?"

Avi looked on with sympathy. "Yes. As I explained to you before, you are not in any trouble here. You did not steal this. Very bad people did a long time ago. Dr. Brindles, would you turn over the painting in your hand?"

Dr. Brindles flipped the painting over and pointed to the brown paper tag that read: "Sicherges durch den Einsatzstab RR, Stabsfuhrung." Avi continued, "That is the Rosenberg mark. Now, this picture here was painted by Vincent van Gogh. The name of the painting is *The Artist on the Road to Tarascon*. Unfortunately, Mr. van Gogh was considered a degenerate artist by the Nazis and some of his works were destroyed. *The Artist on the Road to Tarascon* was considered a degenerate piece and was thought to have been destroyed when the Allied forces bombed the Kaiser-Friedrich Museum in 1945. But I'm happy to say, you two ladies proved history wrong. The painting still exists."

"How do you fit into all of this?" I asked.

"It's simple, really. Israeli intelligence is tracking these paintings."

Avi drew his chair closer to mine. I could feel the pheromones rising again. Dang, this man had a raw attractiveness that I couldn't explain. He was rugged, not classically handsome, and he had these deep brown deliberate eyes that I found mesmerizing.

"But you should know it is not just about the paintings. I am tracking the man who kept the paintings in storage, Mr. Ernst Strickland, which, by the way, is not his real name. The family name was Steichenhahl and it was anglicized to Strickland. This is where your friend Freddie comes in. Freddie bought the storage unit, and I introduced myself to him. He agreed to help me retrieve the paintings for a fee, of course."

Karrie could not control herself even when she simply heard Freddie's name. "Of course, he would charge you a fee. He was a cheap creep—"

"Karrie, please. Just let the man finish."

Avi laughed. "We planned to meet in August, but he was murdered before I could get to him. Freddie was probably killed because

Strickland wants his art back. This man was responsible for killing thousands of people, and Strickland's son? No better than the father. To kill one unimportant junk seller like our Freddie? That would be nothing at all to a man like this. I'd been going to Columbia Meadows market quietly for six months. But by the time I found Freddie, it was too late. Strickland knew he had the art."

Karrie leaned over and whispered loudly. "Tell Avi that somebody's been trying to kill you."

"No!"

"Ladies, again, I am right here and I can hear everything. Who is trying to kill you?"

I wasn't sure if I wanted to actually get into this. I didn't know who to trust. How did I know that he wasn't trying to kill *me*? I was so confused. I decided that I would tell him. Maybe it would make a difference.

"Freddie owned a house in Colts Neck. Karrie and I found some of art there. While we were in the house, someone tried to shoot me using .50 caliber bullets. Blew the walls apart."

He chuckled. "Mustn't have been a very good shot. You are still here with us, yes? If they hit you with that kind of a round, you would lack a limb or a head."

"Obviously they missed!" Karrie interjected. "We lived to tell the tale. Do you want to see another painting or not?"

"Madam, I would like to see all the paintings, the sculpture, anything you have. This art belongs to the world, or else it belongs to families of holocaust survivors. Who knows about this art besides the two of you, Ms. Sanchez?"

I ran the names through my head quickly: Karrie, Iceman, and possibly Mr. Queecy, but I wasn't sure. Queecy told me that he was still trying to unravel Freddie's messy finances. "I'm not sure, David…I mean Avi. The New Jersey State Police know, I'll give you the name of the officer handling this case. I gave him all the art I found in the storage locker. It's locked up in an evidence locker. It's safe."

Karrie jumped in. "Now wait just a minute here. How do we know *you're* legit? How do we know that you're not some shady art dealer poser?"

He stepped in front of Karrie and dropped down on one knee. There was something so humbling yet very sensual about this move that I would've believed him if Avi told me he was the King of Canada. He gently took Karrie's hand in his and said, "Mrs. Langston, I care only about returning what belongs to people who suffered greatly for it. And I only want to catch a killer, an aged madman who thinks he has escaped justice. I am no poser, and I am asking, begging for your help." With that he gently kissed her hand, released it, and stood up.

With a somewhat shocked yet vacant look in her eyes she said, "Okay, I believe you. Roxie, why don't you show him the other painting as well?"

I picked up the other painting that I had brought with me. It had that same brown paper mark on the back. Unlike the van Gogh, it was signed. I handed it to Dr. Brindles. His eyes smiled as he began to explain who the artist was.

"This painting was done by a man named Josef Nassy, a black expatriate of Jewish descent. He was arrested in Belgium, and he and his wife were placed in an internment camp in upper Bavaria. During that time he painted about, oh, two hundred paintings. Many are with the Holocaust Museum in D.C."

"I guess now you have two hundred and one with this painting by Mr. Nassy." I looked at Dr. Brindles and Avi. "Could I talk to my friend alone for a minute?"

Both men nodded and left the room. I noticed that Dr. Brindles took the van Gogh with him.

I spoke in hushed tones to Karrie, figuring the room was probably bugged. "This is scaring me. I can only assume that this man Steichenhahl, Strickland or whatever his name is, is some kind of homicidal maniac, He's going to come after me because he still thinks I stole Freddie's paintings."

Karrie looked thoughtful. "That's a definite possibility. I say we give them all the art and make a public announcement that all the art has been donated. That way the whole world knows that you don't have it anymore."

"How can that keep me alive? If this murderer's out there, he's going to think I sold the art and made a lot of money off his ill-gotten gains. What am I going to do if this guy comes after me again? What do I say to this jerk? 'Please don't kill me 'cause I don't have your stuff.' This all makes sense now. The guy that killed Freddie is trying to kill me." I watched as Karrie sat up very straight.

"There is only one thing you can do. You are obviously surrounded by two very handsome men. Both are packing heat...heat in more ways than one," she said as she winked.

"And?"

"If I were you, I think I'd pick one and make him my boyfriend. This may work to your advantage in staying alive."

I sighed. "Staying alive. Sounds like that old song by the Bee Gees. What about Picasso's sketchbook?"

"Let's hold off on that one," she whispered. "We need to get back to the Colts Neck house."

Boyfriend?

I hadn't had a real boyfriend since that Texas lawyer. After getting my emotions obliterated by him, I wasn't really interested in taking up with anyone. But technically I was living the dream: a choice of two potential lovers, each of whom made me weak at the knees in different ways. Which one do I show an interest in? Iceman or Avi, the mysterious foreign intelligence officer? With me and men, it's always been feast or famine, with the famine usually accompanied by a plague of locusts and frogs after the relationship tanks. In this case, both men were feasts, exemplary specimens of fine sexual dining. Too much thinking.

I needed a vodka martini or Karrie's almond cheesecake with caramel topping. I was convinced that medical science has not fully understood the medicinal properties of expensive booze or a good piece of home baked cake.

I went outside to tell Dr. Brindles that they could come back into the room. I told them that I would be calling Freddie's estate lawyer, Alfonse Queecy, to let him know that we would be turning certain items over to the FBI and the New Jersey State Police. I had to try to take some control over this yet again bizarre situation.

"We'll leave the paintings we brought today. I'm going to have to call my lawyer, Mr. Alfonse Queecy, and tell him all about the paintings. I'm sure that we can work something out and have the paintings turned over to you. I agree with you, Avi. These works of art belong to the world."

"Roxie, how did you and Mrs. Langston get into the city today?" Avi asked.

"How do trains, planes, and automobiles sound? Actually just two trains."

"Let me drive you and Mrs. Langston home. It's the least I can do. You both have had a long day."

"Deal. It really has been a long day." I looked at Dr. Brindles. "Can we go home now?"

"Absolutely, my dear. Have your attorney contact me or Agent Antares directly."

****

After leaving the two paintings with the auction house, Avi pulled up on West 21st Street. in a Crown Vic. I had this feeling that it was going to be another wild ride, just like the one I had taken previously with Pete Carsen. I'm convinced that most police officers know only two speeds: fast and faster. Driving at breakneck speed, we flew across town, drove through the Lincoln Tunnel, and then hit the New Jersey Turnpike. This time I put Karrie in the front seat. Despite the odometer hitting eighty-five miles an hour, she sat serenely in the front seat next to Avi. He dropped her off at her home, then turned to me.

"Why do you and I not get a drink?"

'Why not?" I responded.

He occasionally switched verbs, mispronounced words like "looking beck" instead of "looking back," and would accent the wrong syllables. But his accent was absolutely charming, and Avi Antares had a certain sincerity that was absolutely intriguing to me.

But like many of the other men I had dated, he had a bad boy quality. Bad boys are for sherry and giggles, certainly not to be taken seriously. As an international intelligence officer, he probably had women stashed all over the world, and a wife back in Tel Aviv. And you know what they say, any port in a storm. I had no intention of becoming the guy's safe harbor. Iceman had definitely gone out of his way to try to keep our relationship professional. It was apparent to me that Avi was not only willing to cross international borders, but invade personal boundaries if he felt like it.

"Can you make a suggestion around here for a nice restaurant?"

I thought for a minute as I looked at my watch. It was past nine, and many of the dinner places in Freehold were already starting to close their kitchens. I could drag him back to the Court Jester, but I had been there so many times lately with Karrie, it was almost embarrassing. I suggested the Metropolitan Café near the Court Jester, where we could still get a late-night supper, and I wouldn't be recognized as a local barfly.

After appetizers, two glasses of Cabernet, filet mignon, and a piece of New York cheesecake split between the two of us, I was so full I was about to burst. I think he was a little amused by my voracious appetite. Little did he know that on any given day, I could eat an entire cow.

"So Avi, this dinner we're having, is it personal or professional? I mean if you took me to dinner just to get more information out of me, I've already told you everything I know. There's nothing left to tell, except that I am willing to turn over all the stolen art to you and the FBI. Tell me about yourself."

He placed both hands on the white linen tablecloth in front of him. "What do you want me to say, darling? You already know my name, and you know that I am an intelligence officer from Israel. I just turned thirty-five. Not to much to tell, really. I grew up in Tel Aviv. I like Bruce Springsteen. He's the Boss in New Jersey, yes?"

"I just have this gut feeling that you know everything about me, and I know absolutely nothing about you except that your name really isn't David Williams."

He looked a bit cautious. "Okay. Listen to this. One could say I am a hunter of sorts."

"You hunt down people and kill them for a living?"

He backed away from the table. I hit a nerve. I watched him as he cocked his head. At first I thought the look was anger or suspicion, until those wonderful full lips parted into a smile. "It's like, how do you say, I can tell you but then I'd have to kill you."

I was washing down the last bit of cheesecake with an ice cold mineral water; when he said the word 'kill,' water sprayed from my mouth like a fountain.

"Sorr-r-y." I gagged. "Didn't mean to pry. Don't kill me. Please. Too young to die."

He gave me that big wonderful smile again. "You know, Roxie Sanchez, I like you, too much. But you," he said pointing a finger, "are a dangerous woman."

"Why am I dangerous?"

"It is rare that people just walk into murders or just happen to inherit stolen art. How do you explain that to me?"

"Avi, I don't know. Very bad luck. Born under a bad sign. Cursed by an old gypsy when I was five. What else can I say? On a different topic, what do you want me to call you now: Avi or David?"

"How about Dave? Real American, yes?"

"Just to clear up a point, I am a woman in danger, not a dangerous woman. Someone tried to break into my apartment and then a week before that, someone tried to shoot me. Getting a little tired of this." I made my index finger and thumb into the sign of a gun and waved it in his face.

"Do you have a gun?"

"No."

"Do you want one?"

"Not really."

"Do you at least have pepper spray?"

"No, but a fortune-teller gave me some belladonna oil to ward off evil spirits."

He reached out and took my hand, staring into my eyes. "You may can kill him with this, but you won't have a chance to do that if he has a gun pointed to your head, yes? A flying bullet moves faster than poison. Powerful grip Let me at least get you some pepper spray. I have some in the car."

I gently pulled my hand away from his powerful grip. "Thanks. I appreciate that. I guess the pepper spray is better than nothing."

"Well I hope if you ever need it, it serves you well." He looked at his watch. "Listen my beautiful girl, I have to go. I'm tired, and the day has just caught up with me."

"Yeah, I could use some shuteye. Going from Monmouth County to New York City, then back to Monmouth County has felt like a really long day. We should get the check."

The waiter came and put the check in the middle of the table. I started digging for my credit card, which I hoped still had some financial room, and placed it inside the check holder.

"Roxie, you didn't tell me you are paying for dinner," he laughed.

"I'm not paying for dinner. I'm paying for my half of the dinner." I opened the check holder and was shocked to see that the dinner had come to $150 without the tip. That's more than I eat in a month.

"Please take your credit card back. This is on me."

Under normal circumstances, I wouldn't have minded that he paid for my dinner. My biggest concern now was that after paying $150 for my Kobe beef and New York cheesecake, I was now going to have to sleep with him. Then I thought again. This man probably has a wife and kids back in the old country. What was I thinking? He probably isn't interested in me anyway. I put my concerns away and let him pick up the tab.

"Thanks, Dave. I really appreciate it."

He nodded. "Do you want to really show me some appreciation?"

Oh crud, I thought. *Here comes the boom, his mojo, getting himself into the zone to make the move on me.*

"How much appreciation?"

He scribbled something on a piece of paper. "Take my number. Help me find the man who's been hiding those paintings for the past fifty years. Deal?"

"You're on."

"Excellent. Now let me drive you home."

That was disappointing. He really wasn't interested in sleeping with me. So this night I would be going home to bed, alone again. Boy, was Karrie going to be disappointed when she heard this.

****

When I came home, I changed my clothes, and lay across the bed. Strange. It was going to be another sleepless night over the Golden Lychee. Physical attraction is always a double-edged sword. It's like you really want the guy to be attracted to you, but then if he comes on too strong, you're always afraid he's going to think you're desperate. I haven't quite figured out how to resolve this issue within myself. All I know is that I was attracted to both Dave and Iceman, and I wasn't sure if attraction to either one would be good for me. As usual, there were no easy choices, just choices.

CHAPTER 12

The next day I was back at the firm. The night before kept lingering in my mind, in addition to the smell of some exotic cologne Dave had worn. As I sat in my little cubicle, the previous night seemed like a whirlwind. New York, a ritzy auction house, a van Gogh, and an Israeli intelligence agent. I still couldn't get over that I had in my possession a van Gogh painting that was thought to have been destroyed back in 1945. Instead it winds up in a forsaken New Jersey storage unit. As things got more complicated, I found that it got harder and harder to pay attention to my daily work. But I needed to keep the lights on, so I did what I could.

I started opening the mail to see what new motions and briefs had come in that the firm's attorneys needed to respond to. We had just gotten a notice of appeal on a trial that Pynchard had won, and I had to turn that over to Mac. He was our appellate guru. I got up to walk towards Mac's office with the notice of appeal, but Mac had just shown his face at my cubicle.

"I just wanted to give you the heads-up," he said. "I overheard a conversation. Pynchard was sitting in his office talking on the phone. He doesn't realize that the walls here are probably thinner than rice paper."

"No one's planning to assassinate me today, are they?"

"I don't think it's that simple."

"W-what?"

"Pynchard was talking about a recent art acquisition."

"So what? I don't care what this man does. I don't care if he collects used lollipops or old twigs for a hobby." I had to stop myself. Poor Mac was just trying to give me some information because he was concerned, and instead I just wanted to rip into Edward Pynchard again. "Mac, I'm sorry. I just get carried away every time I hear that man's name. He's just been so mean to me."

"Just hear me out. He talked about – and I couldn't really hear the rest of the conversation too well – but he talked about getting art off the boat."

"Oh my God."

"Did you know about this?"

"The guy at Parsells Marina told Karrie and me that he had heard that some people were at the marina looking at the *Bearded Lady* before Karrie and I got to the boat. I can only think that that must've been Pynchard." I sighed in disgust. "What a miserable man."

"Can't disagree with you on that one. But is he really supposed to be poking around down there? I mean, for all intents and purposes, you inherited that boat. What's he doing down there?"

"I don't know. But I can tell you this much – none of this can be very good. Thanks for the heads-up."

"You're welcome, Roxie. I'm really sorry the news couldn't have been better." Mac and I looked up together as Pynchard exited his office and came toward me. Then Mac began chattering. "At this point, I am sure that you understand why I really think we need to get those interrogatories done by next week, don't you think? Anyway, we can talk about this later."

"I'll get on it right away. I actually had started to do it, but then I got caught up on other work."

With that, Mac walked away.

I noticed that Pynchard was wearing a particularly somber suit that day. I had no idea if he was going to court to argue a motion or attend a funeral. His suit was one of those deep, deep blacks that if you were to get even a single gray hair on the shoulder, it would be noticeable from a mile away. But Pynchard was so vain about his looks, I was surprised if a hair would even be there. I'm sure he vacuumed himself regularly.

He brushed passed me and directed me to go to his office.

"My office now Roxie."

Immediately I got the usual sickening feeling in the pit of my stomach that a command from Pynchard always caused. Going into his office was walking into a predator's bay. He was the shark, I was the minnow. The fact that he wanted me to come into his office today, after learning that perhaps he had made an unannounced appearance at the marina and boarded the *Bearded Lady*, made me wonder. What did he have in store for me? None of this left me feeling very good. He gestured me into his office and I followed.

"Roxie, I just wanted to know how your estate stuff was going. I know this firm represents you, but Mr. Blackwood has been kind of mum on the whole situation. So tell me. What's been happening?"

"Mr. Pynchard, can I ask you a question first? What is your interest in this estate?"

"It is merely an intellectual curiosity on my part. After all, it's not often that a paralegal inherits an estate from an eccentric millionaire about whom she knows nothing. I also couldn't help but overhear that you reported being shot at. Aren't you a little worried that someone will come after you again?"

I could feel my blood pressure rising. My cheeks started to get red, flushed with anger at the nerve of Pynchard making a statement like that. I mean, who the heck was he? What did he mean by this intellectual curiosity? I have an intellectual curiosity about how much money Bill Gates has in his personal checking account, but if I met the man, I certainly wouldn't ask him that question. Nervy, really nervy to ask me about Freddie's estate. It wasn't like we were friends. He was my employer, and an employer who basically tolerated me the way someone tolerated a head cold. He couldn't complain about my work because my work speaks for itself. But working for him, I learned in fairly short order that he's the kind of guy that if you made one misstep – the stamp is put on the envelope upside down or– the paper clips were set to the left corner of the document, not the right corner- you became his target. I didn't want to let on how much I knew. I didn't want to tell him about the art in the storage unit, the Israeli intelligence officer, and the fact that I was planning to go back to the boat and the Colts Neck house. The less Pynchard knew about my intentions, the better off I was.

"Well, you know, the police are involved now. I have to call Mr. Queecy because I have some questions. But no, I'm not worried. You think I should be, Mr. Pynchard?"

"Only you know if you should be worried or not. I can't tell you what to think or what to concern yourself about."

"I don't know, Mr. Pynchard. I guess I'm just curious why you're asking."

"Roxie, the firm is representing you gratis on this whole estate thing. I think that I'm entitled to inquire as to what you know or do not know about certain assets in the estate, like the art."

"I don't really know much. But I did hear that people were at that boat."

I noticed that he raised an eyebrow when I said that. I'd like to think that he was slightly nervous, but I knew that that wasn't really his nature. He was plotting. I felt in my gut that he was at that boat removing things. I wasn't really sure how to play this one. I kind of felt like I wanted to toy with him a little bit, but I had to keep in mind that I had to look at this creep every day. I couldn't toy too much with one of my bosses.

"What are you talking about? Did someone actually see people moving things from the boat?"

Strange answer. I never said anything about people moving things *from* the boat. All I said is that people were *at* the boat. I was thinking that right about now was the time to call Mr. Parsells and see if he had found out anything from those kids who saw people leaving the *Bearded Lady*. I decided to play it stupid.

"Oh, I don't know, Mr. Pynchard. I guess I'm kind of confused. Do you need anything else? I've really got to get some stuff out for Mac."

"You are dismissed." With that last remark, he slammed a legal pad on the desk. Something I said must've irritated him. But at that particular point, I didn't care.

****

I ran over to Karrie's house after work. I was planning to call the marina to see who exactly had been on that boat besides Karrie and me. As usual, my best friend was one step ahead of me. She had made the phone call, and I got the answer we both expected.

"I called Jimmy Parsells, and he told me that his marina assistants are all Boy Scouts who are trying to earn sailing badges. To my mind, it means they're probably pretty honest kids."

"Okay. Did they see anything?"

"Well, what Jimmy said was that – and mind you, I had to listen to a whole story about his gallbladder surgery and his sailing trip to Key Largo. Good grief, he's told me that story a hundred times…"

"Karrie, focus!"

"Well, he finally told me that the kids saw a well-dressed man with dark hair and a mustache along with two well-dressed women going onto the boat. Then he said that the kids said it looked as though they were taking big square things off the boat."

"Karrie, do you know what that means? We got sloppy seconds. I bet that was Pynchard with Freddie's two sisters, Jule Mustergrave and Lorelei Kranz. I better call Mr. Queecy."

"I have a better idea. Why don't you call Detective Baines or your new friend, the nice Israeli intelligence officer?"

I smiled, thinking to myself how Iceman or Dave would be the last people Edward Pynchard would want to see.

CHAPTER 13

Saturday Karrie and I were back at the market doing our thing. We went in separate vehicles today because we were each loaded up to the gills with new items to sell.

A friend of Karrie's, who had relocated off to a fifty-five and over active adult community, had a whole bunch of 1960s collectibles that she wanted Karrie to sell, many pieces of which Karrie purchased outright. She also had a large collection of vintage costume jewelry by designers like Elsa Schiaparelli and Miriam Haskell. We hadn't had any time to sort and price out all of the costume jewelry, so we were really playing it by ear when a customer asked how much something was. I knew if I said anything less than twenty dollars on the designer stuff, Karrie would be giving me her famous stink eye.

Fishy came wandering over with a bunch of daylilies whose stem ends were wrapped in tin foil. He was headed in Karrie's direction. She couldn't have been happier if I had stuck a shard of glass in her big toe. I watched as Fishy McClure hobbled over with the half-dead daylilies, which he had probably plucked off the side of the road.

"Morning, ladies," said Fishy as he handed Karrie the flowers. "Wondering if there's any news about our dearly departed Freddie."

Karrie took the flowers and put them aside. "No news, Mr. Fish. Thanks for the flowers. How's business today?"

"Well, sold the bunch of lures, but there's a lot of lookie loos."

"What's a lookie loo?"

I interjected. "Lookie loos are people who make you show everything you have and buy nothing."

Karrie nodded. "Ah yes, we had quite a few of those last week."

From the look on Karrie's face, I could see that she had had enough of Fishy and wanted him to leave. Personally, I didn't want to be rude to the guy but we had a lot of stuff, we were still setting up, and old Fish loved to chat. And it seemed he always liked to chat when *he* had no business. We were busy. Fish had to move along. I looked over at Karrie. I knew what was coming.

She batted her eyes and got flirty with Fishy, then using a more familiar form of his real name was actually Albert McClure, she cooed, "You know Bertie, I would love to talk to you, but this little girl here and I are just *so* busy. Can I drop by your table a little later?"

I looked at Fish; he looked as though he was going to have a coronary, but it would be a *mort heureuse* – a happy death with a big smile on his face. He couldn't have been more conciliatory at the prospect of a visit from Karrie.

"Oh, my dear," he said, "make sure you stop over later. Perhaps we can grab a bite to eat, a little steak between us?" He winked.

I thought I was gonna get nauseous. She kept batting her eyes. If the butterfly kisses had flapped any harder, her eyelids would have required their own flight path over LaGuardia. With every blink, Fishy's ear-to-ear grin grew in length until his already thin lips became a giant string bean pasted across his face. I had to hand it to Karrie. For an old gal, she had the touch. She never agreed to meet him later. She simply made googly eyes, making him believe she would go over. He hobbled away a happier old man.

"Roxie, I want to go back to the Colts Neck house today when we're done at the market."

"I'm worried. Queecy told me not to go back there. Don't you remember that little matter of the shooting when we were there? Do we really want to return to the scene of the crime?"

She gave me a big wide smile. "There's not a doubt in my mind we should go back. But this time we're going back with a little protection."

"What kind of protection? All I have is the pepper spray Dave gave me."

"Come here." She gestured me over to her car and opened the trunk. Inside I saw a small metal strongbox with a big old padlock on it. Karrie took out the key from her purse and opened the strongbox. I looked inside.

"A cap gun? That's what you want to use to protect us? A cap gun? This is almost as bad as the water pistol I tried to use on the person who broke into my apartment."

"Don't be silly." She picked up the small gun. "This, my dear, is a two-shot derringer. My ex-husband bought it for me when we were selling a lot in Manhattan."

"You're making me nervous. Don't you have to have a license or something?"

"It's called a permit, Roxie. And yes, I have one. Just not a permit to carry. New Jersey's very strict about those things, you know." She wagged a finger.

"Well, if you can't carry it, how are you going to take the gun into the Colts Neck house with me tonight?"

"Oh, I keep it in my purse all the time. Besides, you and me, who's going to know?"

Once again I found the palm of my hand slapping against the middle of my forehead, almost pushing my eyeballs out the back of my head. There was no arguing with this woman.

****

It was a good night to break into a house, moonless and dark.

We drove down the long winding road back to Freddie's Colts Neck house and parked the car a distance away. Under cover of darkness, the two of us trotted toward the derelict mansion armed with pepper spray and a two-shot derringer...which I was going to make believe Karrie wasn't carrying in her oversized Coach purse. Like good half-baked burglars, we were dressed from head to toe in black, including ski caps. Karrie even had a couple of ski masks if we needed them. Since we weren't exactly going to knock off a bank, I thought the ski masks were a bit much. Karrie also had a big black canvas sack flung over her shoulder. We were reverse Santa Clauses: going in with sacks and taking out presents instead of leaving them.

It was going to be one heck of a night.

On tiptoes we jogged toward the house and tried to make a quiet ascent up rickety porch stairs carefully stepping over the third step I'd previously fallen through. But it didn't work; the wooden steps constantly betrayed us. It was *creak-creak-creak* all the way up. I paused at the top of the stairs and said, "Here we are again. Slum, sweet slum."

I had learned my lesson the first time so I made sure I spoke to the electric company and had the electricity turned on.. . While we were inside the something with the semblance of a vestibule, I saw a car parked in the back of the house. But as we approached the house, we stopped dead in our tracks. I couldn't believe it . I could see clearly through a back window– there was a car parked outside the house, and I knew who it belonged to. I certainly didn't expect them to show up here. I looked Karrie straight in the eye.

"Is that derringer in your purse loaded?"

"Yes, dear, of course it is. What would be the point otherwise?"

"Give it to me."

"Since when did you decide to play Yosemite Sam?"

"Since I recognize the creep that's marching through my house!"

I would not have believed it if I hadn't seen it with my own eyes. There it was in all its familiar glory. A banged-up red Volkswagen beetle with a poorly drawn dragon decal that looked like it was vomiting after a bout of bad General Tso's chicken. I was furious.

"Should we go around the back?" Karrie whispered.

"No. Going right through the front door. And I changed my mind – I don't need the gun. I know this crook"

She raised an eyebrow. "You sure about that?"

The locks had been changed on the Colts Neck house. I used my key to open the front door and quietly made my entrance. When I flipped the light switch on, the thieves stopped dead in their tracks. The two young men looked like they had just seen a ghost.

"Li, how could you? Does your father know you're here?"

There was my landlord's son, Li, and a friend with arms full of pottery, silverware, and a piece of bronze statuary. I was fit to be tied.

"Well? What have you got to say for yourself?" I opened up my cell phone and pretended that I was going to dial 9-1-1. I watched as Li carefully put the items he was carrying down on the floor and raised his hands.

"Look Roxie, I can explain. I really didn't know what to do. Freddie had borrowed about three grand from my father and he blew it all that some dump called the Taj Mahal in Atlantic City. Freddie kept promising to pay him back but never did. The restaurant hasn't been doing so good, so I thought I'd take a look around the house and see if there was anything that I might be able to take back to pay Freddie's gambling debt. The restaurant isn't doing so good, Roxie. I was hoping to maybe finds some stuff and sell it on Ebay."

I noticed beads of sweat across his forehead. "Dad needs the money. Don't be mad at my father... And if my mother ever found out that my father lent Freddie this much money, she'd kill him. I was just trying to help out my dad." He squeezed his hands together. "You know how cheap he is."

"Li, regardless of how cheap he is – and yeah, your father is a tightwad and cheapskate – you have no right to break into a person's house and exact your own justice to pay a debt. I could have you arrested. You're a good kid. And you're still in the engineering program at Stevens Institute in Hoboken, right?"

I watched as the young man with the spiked hair with green tips looked down at the floor with embarrassment. "Yeah."

"Something like this can get you kicked out of college, Li."

Li looked up tearfully. "You're not going to call the police on me and my friend, are you? Eddie goes to Stevens, too."

I sighed and closed my eyes. "No, I'm not going to call the police. But I want something out of this. Tell me about Freddie's gambling."

"All I know is that he and my father used to hit Atlantic City pretty regularly. And I think the whole money borrowing thing was a regular occurrence between them. Sometimes Dad would borrow money from Freddie, sometimes Freddie would borrow money from Dad."

Karrie inserted her two cents. "Son, how long has this little gambling party been going on with Freddie and your father?"

"Wow, I'm eighteen now, and I remember Freddie and my dad going to AC when I was still in high school. They've been doing it for several years. And there was never a problem. But this last time Freddie's into my dad for three grand, and then…well, you know what happened."

"Yes, Freddie is now pushing up daisies, and he can't pay your father back," Karrie snapped. "Do us both a favor. Put the items you have in your hands on the floor and just go. Roxie and I will forget the whole incident and move on. Just don't come back here."

"Are you going to tell my father?" Li looked at me with incredibly sad eyes. Either he was the best actor in the world or else this young kid truly knew the meaning of the word remorse. He made a mistake. I didn't feel that it was my job to ruin his life.

"No. I'm not. But I never want to see you back here." I thought for a minute. "What exactly were you going to take from this dump?"

"Me and Eddie found these paintings. And I found this bronze statue. We thought if we could sell it on eBay we might make some money to pay back my dad."

I watched as Karrie looked at the paintings and the bronze sculptures; she was probably thinking the same thing I was thinking. Neither one of us knew enough about art to determine if these were priceless stolen works of art or if they were stuff you could buy and sell at a flea market.

One of the statues, I recognized immediately. Old Freddie had had a miniature version of Rodin's *The Kiss*, a sculpture of a two lovers drawn up in a passionate embrace. Freddie claimed his was a bronze sculpture, an "extra" sculpture released from a museum that he purchased from a private collector. He wanted a thousand bucks for it. It sat on his table for a year with no takers. I remembered it.

Bronze anything is usually worth some money. Even if it wasn't a museum piece, the bronze would've been worth something either for artistic or melt value. I took a magnet to that statue one day and had trouble prying the magnet loose. True bronze is not magnetic. The statue wasn't bronze. Another one of Freddie's fake museum pieces!

"Okay, look. I will talk to Mr. Queecy. Once we sell this house and straighten things out, the state can pay your father back. You'll need to show me proof. But coming in here and taking stuff isn't the answer. Follow me?"

Li nodded. "Yeah. We're good." After putting all the items he was planning to sell on eBay on the floor, the two young men quietly left. I heard the broken muffler on the Volkswagen beetle with the ugly dragon decal as it took off.

"Roxie, gambling is a good reason for murder. I mean, who knows how much money Freddie was really into your landlord for? His son says about three thousand dollars – it could actually be twenty thousand dollars. You don't really know."

"I didn't think about it that way. I'm going to call Baines. You're right. This could be a motive for murder."

Karrie and I picked up the pieces of art that Li and Eddie left behind. All of this stuff had to be accounted for. Queecy would not be pleased that we were back at the house, but I thought it was a good thing that we showed up. I had this vision that the next person appearing at Freddie's house would be Pynchard.

****

I woke sleeping handsome up.

A drowsy voice answered the phone, and from the sound of it, I had the impression that he was a bit hung over. He released a deep moan that sounded as though it came from the bowels of the earth. I envisioned his long, muscular biceps stretching over his head, reaching like a big old tomcat that just came in from a night on the prowl. I half wished he was prowling around in my bed.

I didn't know how happy he was going to be to hear from me, but I needed to tell him what I had just learned.

"Baines?"

"Sanchez? To what do I owe the pleasure of this phone call? I was in the middle of a dream with naked women massaging me with lavender. And guess what? You were in it."

"Really?"

He laughed. "Nah, if you were in it that would be a nightmare."

"Thanks a lot. Since I'm annoying you, I think I'm just going to hang up the phone and not talk about the motivation for Freddie's murder."

"Okay, Madam Sherlock, what do you have?"

"I'm here at Freddie's house–"

"I thought I told you to stay away from that place. Now that we know that Freddie was in possession of stolen Nazi art, anybody going there could be a target. You are taking your life in your hands. I know I'm going to be sorry I asked, but is Karrie with you?"

"Oh, she's here. We're protected. She's carrying a two-shot derringer.

"Oh great. Calamity Jane with Annie Oakley carrying a derringer." He sighed. "Sanchez, someone aimed at you with .50 caliber bullets, and blew out the walls. You probably couldn't even crack two shots off with that gun. Anyway, you need to get out of there. Tell me about your theory of Freddie's murder first."

"When we came to the house, we found that we weren't alone. Two college kids were in the house, taking out art and other things. We caught them red-handed."

"Did you have them arrested?"

"Don't be mad at me when I tell you the answer. No, I didn't. I recognized one of the kids – it was my landlord's son."

"What is your landlord's son doing in Freddie's house?"

"He told me that Freddie owed his father some money. Couple of thousand bucks. Apparently they were regulars in Atlantic City."

I notice that Baines' ears perked up. "Really? You like your landlord for this murder?"

"Well, no. I mean, I guess anything is possible, but I don't think my landlord would do something like this. But I thought that it was an interesting connection with the murder."

"I see. I want to think about this for a bit. Now, you mind if I go back to sleep?"

"Have you talked to David about the artwork?"

"Yeah. Too tired to discuss it right now. I'll call you tomorrow. Now get out of that house!"

"Bye."

There was no way I was leaving the house. Karrie and I still had other things to check out. I kept rolling over and over in my head that gambling may have been a possible motivation for this crime. But something still didn't sit right with me. The whole art thing really bothered me. I didn't understand why Freddie had involved himself in stolen art. I thought he was simply a harmless junk seller, sort of like the rest of the dealers down at Columbia Meadows. But apparently there was a whole other side to this guy that I didn't know about, including his wealth, his personal relationships, and more importantly I now knew he was an inveterate gambler who hung out with my landlord.

Things just kept getting stranger and stranger. I wondered what would happen next, and I hoped that it wouldn't involve me taking a bullet.

We went upstairs into Freddie's bedroom. It looked like a scene from that television show *Hoarders*. Like the kitchen, there were half eaten cartons of Chinese take-out, empty pizza boxes, wrappers from McDonald's, and empty bags from Taco Bell. It was inconceivable that Freddie ever ate anything that was remotely healthy. If the knife to the chest didn't kill him, his cholesterol would have. I opened up a nightstand drawer and found a lot of tagged sterling silver jewelry. Holding the bag up, I waved it in Karrie's face.

"Look what I found. Rings, pins, and a couple of necklaces." I looked through the little plastic baggie they were stored in. "Good stuff here. It's all marked .925. Sterling."

"Impressive." She looked at the jewelry through the plastic baggie. "A cameo, sterling silver brooch, two filigree necklaces. I'm surprised the old bastard had such good taste."

I frowned as I jammed the silver in my purse. "I've been keeping a list of everything that we've found in this house and in the storage unit. Have to be legit."

"Why tell Mr. Queecy about the jewelry? He's never gonna know. Just put it in your purse and be done with it. I mean after all, Freddie left you with this stuff. It's yours."

"I know. But if I'm going to be sued by Freddie's sisters, I really can't take any of this stuff until the estate is settled."

"Not to be Nelly Negative, but if this stuff is all stolen Nazi art, there may not be much of an estate left by the time your friend David gets a hold of it. They're just a few little pieces of silver jewelry. I suggest you take it and no one's the wiser."

"Not doing it, Karrie. Playing it by the book here."

"Fiddlesticks!"

"Sh-h-h-! I hear something."

I ran over to the window and saw a car with its lights turned off creeping up the gravel road toward the house. I looked at Karrie.

"Someone is sneaking up the driveway."

"At least whoever it was didn't shoot at us."

"Let's get out of here before something happens. I have a bad feeling."

"Me too. You know, I'm too old for all this, this misadventure."

"Really? Really? Knee deep in the muddy and now you feel old?"

She raised an eyebrow. "Well, not *that* old, I am not frail you know." She pulled the derringer out of her purse. "C'mon, let's get 'em. Before they get us."

"Are you crazy? That Derringer is no match for a .50 caliber bullet!"

Suddenly my seventy-plus friend bolted down the stairs and made a dash for the door like her hair was on fire. Holding the derringer above her head, she raced outside like a twenty year old, ready to shoot anything that threatened her. I watched her rear end run out the door. I couldn't believe my eye, and it begged questions.

What is it? Why is it? How come it's running with a loaded gun?

Nobody pays me enough to be this lady's best friend. Then a second thought popped into my head. Nobody pays me for this at all.

I followed her out the door, and I immediately recognized the car. It was Baines. He exited the Crown Vic that drove slowly down the road. Baines wore a sweat suit, the one he was probably sleeping in when I called him. This man was absolutely amazing. He was one of those people who looked good in anything. I bet I could even throw a burlap sack on him, and he could still make the cover of *GQ* magazine.

He looked annoyed. "Well, well, well. What have we here? I thought I told the two of you to stay away from this place. Do I have to get a restraining order?"

"Now Baines, we're just trying to help you out. Who knows what clues we may find in this house?"

"You two were not put on this earth to find clues for a homicide." He looked at Karrie and began walking toward her. "Mrs. Langston, I am so surprised and disappointed in you." "I'm sure you don't mind if I take this." He gently removed the derringer from her hands.

Karrie blushed. "Oh detective, I am just a poor elderly senior citizen trying to assist this lonely young woman in handling an estate that, quite frankly, is in deplorable condition. I'm not here to hurt anyone. You understand, don't you?" She threw some butterfly kisses in his direction. I wanted to tell her not to bother, but I figured that she was doing the best she could under the circumstances.

He tried to contain a smile. "Yes, I know, Mrs. Langston, but I am concerned about the safety of you and your little friend over here. Think for a minute. Your friend Freddie buys the farm with a knife in his chest. You two go to this house and someone fires a few warning shots over your heads. Somewhere out there, there's a killer. It's my duty to make sure that the body count doesn't pile up. So I'm warning you. Stay away from this house." He looked at me. "That means you too, Sanchez."

"If that's what you want, Detective Baines. Karrie and I will go home, and we won't come back here."

My late mother always said to me, "If nothing else, you can always be polite." And that's exactly what I was, little Miss Polite.

Yeah, right.

****

I called Dave the next day and told him about my strange conversation with Pynchard. I also told him that the owner of Parsells

Marina had informed me that people who sounded an awful lot like Pynchard and Freddie's two sisters were moving art off the boat.

"And when did this occur?"

"A few days ago."

"And who is this, this Pynchard? A friend, eh?"

"No, no, not at all. We hate each other. He's my boss."

"You are a paralegal, yes?"

"Yes."

"He's a lawyer then."

"Uh-huh. And just so you know, he likes me about as much as a dose of malaria."

I heard a heavy sigh on the other end of the phone. "I'll look into it. Just be careful."

CHAPTER 14

It's not easy trying to live a normal life when you have a police officer and a foreign intelligence agent telling you to stay away from places and to look over your shoulder. It was Friday night and I was packing up for Saturday morning at Columbia Meadows with Karrie. She had telephoned me earlier to brag that she had scored a huge lot of Roseville pottery, including a large Donatello pedestal vase and a bowl with cherubs for a ridiculous price at a morning garage sale.

"I saw these twelve pieces of Roseville, really good stuff, the genuine article, and I tried not to look too excited. I got the whole lot for fifty bucks, including the large pedestal vase."

"How the heck did you manage to pull that one off? I would think at least one of the vases would cost fifty dollars alone. Fess up, girlfriend. How did you get twelve pieces of vintage Roseville so cheap?"

"The price was the last vestige of a scorned man's dignity. He's an engineer and his wife walked out on him for Enrico, the heating and air conditioning man."

"Well, at least she'll never be too hot or too cold."

"Oh yes." Karrie chortled. "Anyway, he knew that she loved her Roseville and she left in a hurry when she ran into Enrico's arms. He told me that it's been months since the divorce was finalized, and she left all this stuff in the garage. He simply couldn't bear to look at anymore, poor fellow, so I took it off his hands. Couldn't leave him with sad memories of a broken heart now, could I?"

I laughed. "Nice! Will I see you tomorrow?"

"Of course, dear." She hung up.

****

The morning weather started off in the low 60s with a slight breeze and no chance of rain. I was happy to be at Columbia Meadows, working with Karrie, trying to keep my mind off Freddie. The unpretentious folk at Columbia Meadows were a welcome sight.

Lingerie Lottie came over to our tables and gave us some of her home-baked blueberry muffins, which were legendary in both size and taste. As I devoured the muffin like it was the last meal I'd ever eat, I kept thinking that I should just rub the muffin all over my hips. That's where it was going to wind up eventually, making my jeans tighter until I had to buy a new pair that would let me breathe. But if at any time I had a misgiving about what I wore at Columbia Meadows, I simply took a look around me. You would not believe what people will wear at the market.

Any time I poured myself into something cut too low or too tight, my mirror screamed "N-o-o-o-o! Don't do it, fool!" But being a quiet student of fashion at the market, I saw hordes of women who did not adhere to the adage, "Just because it comes in your size, doesn't me you should wear it." Chubby ladies donned Spandex cargo pants, wearing midriff tops made of sausage casing that allowed rolls of skin to flow out like ocean waves.

The men were no better. If they weren't wearing a size XXL T-shirt, their protuberant guts under snug T-shirts made them look pregnant. I saw men who looked like they were expecting twins, and one fellow, as round as he was tall, had to be the first octo-dad. It was as though a bunch of circus midgets were trying to punch their way out of a tent that was too small.

Truth be told, I was jealous. Each woman managed to have a spouse on her arm to protect her, unlike me. Okay, maybe the men had no teeth and looked like escapees from the Ape House at the Bronx Zoo, but at least they had someone.

What did I have? How many nothings did I have? Let me count them all.

Okay, I had the estate of a dead guy whose life I had no interest in. I had artwork that was stolen by the Nazis. I used to actually like my job at the firm, until Pynchard came along. I sighed. Karrie must've noticed that I was in a different world, so she decided to say something.

"I know things are difficult right now, but you always have to be thankful for the things that you have."

"I keep trying to figure out what that is. I mean, I guess that in the end this whole estate thing will work out. I feel bad about Freddie. Who would want to see him dead? And then there are the sisters that threatened to sue me. That's not too comforting."

"Let the police figure out who killed Freddie. That's not your job. You just have to be concerned about who was shooting at you. At least you have those two law enforcement guys looking after you."

"Yeah, right."

I noticed Karrie looking elsewhere. "Looks like we have a customer." She pinched my cheek. "Now cheer up. That's always a happy thing, particularly if you make a nice big fat sale."

I watched as a young woman with a toddler tagging along came up to our table. I thought that she was probably looking for toys for her little one. I would have to direct her to Bug Eye Betty, because toys were not something Karrie and I sold. She gave me a big smile.

"You have such lovely things," she stated.

"Thank you. If you see anything you like, I can give you a really good deal on it."

"Do you buy merchandise as well?"

"Sure do. What do you have?"

"I have something very special that I think you'll really want. I was told your name is Roxanne Sanchez, correct?"

There was something about the way she said my name that made me feel uncomfortable. I nodded.

The woman reached into her pocket and handed me a thick envelope. Then she turned and smiled. "You've just been served with process, Ms. Sanchez. Thank you and have a nice day." She grabbed her toddler and started walking away. Karrie yelled after her.

"Gee, I guess you couldn't get a more acceptable job! Don't ever come back to our tables!"

I opened the envelope. I immediately was struck by the name of the firm listed on behalf of the plaintiff. McAdoo and Aster.

Freddie's crackpot sisters had managed to retain a nice top-flight, very expensive Newark firm that I could never afford to retain even if I were going to be indicted for murder. A cheap lawyer in that joint was $385 an hour. I started skimming through the complaint. It appears that Jule Mustergrave and Lorelei Kranz had filed a complaint in Chancery Court seeking to restrain me from any further activity in Freddie's estate and claiming that I somehow had "undue influence" over Freddie because we both worked at Columbia Meadows market. They were full of it. As I read each count in the complaint, I grew angrier and angrier. I turned to Karrie.

"Can you believe this crap? I hardly knew the man. I gave him coffee and helped him jump start his car in the rain. They can have the whole estate! I don't care! Somebody can go and shoot at *them*!"

"Take a deep breath. Think about this for a minute. You're not alone. You have your firm representing you against them. We now know that Freddie was involved in some pretty dark transactions. You had nothing to do with that. I guess the sisters can't get over the fact that their brother despised the ground they walked on. Jealousy, that's all. Pay no attention to those stupid women. Monday, you walk in that office, you go straight in to the senior partner, and you hand in this complaint. Let them deal with it. This isn't personal, Roxie. This is about two women who thought their millionaire brother would leave them all his money, once he took the proverbial dirt nap. It didn't happen and now they're mad. None of this, absolutely none of this, is any fault of yours."

What a wonderful friend Karrie was! I don't know what I'd do without her. "Yeah, that's exactly right. I'm gonna walk into the firm on Monday, hand these papers to the senior partner, and let them deal with it. I am, like, so done with this whole mess. As far as I'm concerned, the two sisters can have the estate." Let them get shot at."

Karrie smiled. "One can only hope," she said sweetly.

CHAPTER 15

Monday could not have come fast enough for me. All weekend long I kept thinking about that hideous complaint with my name plastered all over it. One count actually accused me of having a romantic interest in Freddie with sexual overtones. I would have rather ripped out my brain stem, carried it to a four-way intersection, and tossed it in front of a Mack Truck rather than crawl in the sack with a man with no teeth. The complaint bordered on defamation. I was the victim here, not them. I never asked for this trouble to be brought to my door.

They would depose me for the lawsuit, which is what happens in all civil lawsuits, and then they would get an earful. They may not have wanted to hear what I had to say. In the limited time I had known Pack Rat Freddie, he never once mentioned he had family at all. And after talking to Jule Mustergrave at his wake, I am sure there was good reason for it. He saw them for what they were: money grubbing and self-centered. I couldn't wait to talk to Mr. Blackwood when I went into the office.

I knew Old Rainey would waltz in at nine forty-five a.m. as usual, probably still nursing the remnants last night's bourbon hangover. I would let them get his coffee, and once I knew he was settled in for the day, I would make my move. I had to talk to him today. I had to talk to him immediately. I needed to know that someone was going to help me out with this nasty lawsuit and not leave me hanging out to dry.

It was nine forty-five a.m. Like clockwork, he waltzed in whistling a Broadway show tune. Today he chose the tune "Memory" from the play *Cats*. I gave it about fifteen minutes. He had his coffee, his *Wall Street Journal,* and he was starting to go over messages from phone calls he needed to return. Knowing Big Al as I did, the messages were probably more related to scheduling golf dates than they were work related. I had to get his attention somewhere between the coffee and his newspaper reading. I saw the opportunity and I took it.

"Mr. Blackwood, do you have a moment?"

He looked up from his messages and gave me a smile. "I always have time for my favorite paralegal. Oh wait, you're my *only* paralegal." He laughed at his joke.

"What can I tell you, Mr. B.? I try to do my best."

"Well, you're a damn good paralegal, and don't let anyone kid you. Come on now. Don't stand in the doorway. Sit down. Relax."

I took a deep breath before sitting down and giving him the papers. "I was working at Columbia Meadows the other day, and I got handed these papers, 'Mustergrave et al. v. Sanchez.' Can you believe this stuff? So glad that the firm has my back on this one."

I watched as the lawyer in Big Al kicked in. He put on his reading glasses and read the entire complaint while I sat there. When I tried to ask him a question, he raised his hand as if to say, "Don't interrupt my thought process."

He appeared to take this whole matter very, very seriously. I watched as he wrote a few notes alongside some of the paragraphs and rubbed his chin, as though he was questioning some of the wording of the complaint. When he was done, he looked up.

"There are very serious accusations here. I completely understand why you are concerned. Let me just ask you this question, and don't take it personally. Did you and Freddie…"

"No!" I yelled. "He was an old guy at the flea market with no teeth and a big beer belly! He barely took a bath!"

Big Al shook his head. "This is a terrible situation, a terrible situation. The sisters are accusing you of undue influence and stealing from Freddie's estate."

"Mr. Blackwood, I barely knew the man. I don't know how much plainer I can get than that. I've told the same story to you, to an Israeli intelligence officer, and a state trooper. I don't know what you want me to tell you."

"Like I said, Roxie, this is a bad situation. And I have the unfortunate duty of informing you that the firm cannot represent you in this matter."

My jaw dropped. "Why?"

"Now I know you're not a lawyer, but I'm sure you understand something called conflict of interest. That's where a lawyer must..."

"Yes, I know what that means. A lawyer must recuse himself from a matter where he has some kind of an interest. You never mentioned you had an interest in Freddie's estate."

"Don't jump to conclusions. I do not have an interest in Freddie's estate. Just this weekend I learned that my soon-to-be ex-wife and Jule Mustergrave sit on the board of directors for an art foundation. I don't think that it's appropriate for my firm to handle this matter. There is an appearance of impropriety issue."

"What am I supposed to do?" I felt tears coming to my eyes, but I was determined not to cry in front of my boss. "I mean, I know how expensive litigation gets and I can't afford an attorney."

"You know, Roxie, you remind me of my daughter."

Yeah, I know how well you get along with your daughter. She stopped speaking to you years ago because you cheated on her mother with your second wife who eventually divorced you for cheating on her with your third wife. Spare me the loving daughter crap.

"My daughter is tough and smart and very single-minded. Sort of like you. But sometimes we have to be more flexible in the face of what life throws at us. We have to think outside the box."

"I don't know what you're talking about."

"Roxie, do you think it might be a good idea for you to just walk away from this estate?"

"Excuse me?"

"Now I'm talking to you like a father, not as an attorney. Let's look at the facts we have here, look at what we know. You work for this firm, and you're clearly underpaid. Right now the firm can't afford to pay you what you're really worth, but things may change in the future. In the meantime you work at a flea market on weekends to make extra money. If you have to defend litigation in Chancery Court, particularly against people of means like the Grant sisters, you won't be able to afford to do that. That's at least a $25,000 retainer and then a $100,000 battle. Nobody takes estate litigation on a contingency basis, I have a small firm here and I certainly can't afford to take this case on, especially where there no guarantee at the end of the road that I'll get paid." He shook his head.

"Risks are too high. We're talking depositions, expert testimony, and really high-price litigation. And let me tell you. McAdoo and Aster's lawyers will outspend you. Roxie, my dear, this may be a fight you can't win because you can't afford to fight it. And what spoils will you find at the end of all this? There may not be much of an estate left. Think about it. The state police and probably an agent from the Mossad have seized the real things of any value: Freddie's stolen art. There is a rickety old house in Colts Neck that you can't afford to fix up and sell, so you'd have to sell it as a knockdown, and since there is not title search yet, you don't know if there are any liens on it. Oh yes, and I forgot about that ridiculous boat, the *Happy Clam*..."

"The *Bearded Lady*, Mr. Blackwood," I interjected, but he just spoke over me.

"...some barnacle barge down at the marina. You will have to get rid of that, and from what I'm told, the boat is worthless. The Colts Neck land is worth more than the actual house, and we know that the Grant sisters intend on fighting you tooth and nail for any money in that estate. Then, of course, Alfonse Queecy, as a lawyer for Freddie's estate, may join in the battle to fight you for the assets, if he believes Freddie was a subject of undue influence by you. Look, I've been litigating for almost forty-five years, and litigation is stressful. By fighting this complaint, you are throwing yourself into a battle you probably can't and won't win. You are a Roman gladiator entering the Coliseum with a wooden sword and a paper shield to fight man-eating lions." He sighed. "The best advice I can offer you as your employer and your friend is that you give up this fight, and let the two miserable women take whatever they can. And good luck with all that."

I was in shock, but I forced myself not to respond. There was something about the whole situation that just didn't seem right. I needed my job. Couldn't afford to tell him to drop dead and walk out the door. Still, I just couldn't believe he was abandoning me at the courthouse steps. Something didn't feel right. Something was off. I put the lid on my emotions for the time being. I needed to think. I needed to get second, maybe even third opinions.

"You know, Mr. Blackwood, you make a lot of sense. But this is a complicated matter, and if you don't mind, I'd like to think about what you said. I take your wise counsel very seriously. A walk away from the situation may not necessarily be a bad thing."

I watched as a smile came across Big Al's face. It was the smile of a man who thought he had smelled victory. I guess he thought the fight was over.

"Good girl, very sensible. Think about it for a few days. I'll do one thing for you; I'll call one of the partners I know at McAdoo and Aster. Tell them what you're thinking and ask for an extension of time to answer the complaint."

"Thank you. I appreciate your assistance. I have to get some papers out for Mac, so if you don't mind, I'll get back to my desk."

"Not at all." Without skipping a beat, he proceeded to pick up the *Wall Street Journal* and start reading. It was as though we never had a conversation at all. Business as usual.

I went to our break room and noticed that we were all out of coffee. This gave me the perfect excuse to walk over to a nearby convenience store and pick up some Maxwell House. It would also give me time to get over the shock of what had just happened to me. I needed to talk to Karrie.

****

After I made the purchase at the convenience store, I frantically dialed Karrie's telephone number. I looked at the time on my cell phone. It was about ten-thirty now, and she was probably at the Handson Salon getting her nails done. She probably wouldn't be too happy to take a telephone call unless it was an emergency. This was an emergency. The phone rang.

"I hope this is real important because my nails are getting airbrushed right now."

"Karrie, the firm is refusing to represent me." I heard the beep of another call coming in and looked down at the cell phone display. "Oh great. There's a call coming in from a restricted number. Hang on a minute." I clicked into the incoming call. "Hello?"

There was a lot of static at the other end of the phone. The caller was either in a dead zone or had a bad connection. I heard a man's voice ask, "This is Roxanna Sanchez, yes? Hello?"

"Who's this?" I wasn't taking any chances after all I had been through. The connection was getting worse, fading in and out. "I can't hear you."

Whatever dead zone the caller was driving through must've cleared up. Then I heard his name as clear as a bell and with a slight German accent, "This is Mr. Albrecht Strickland. I believe that you have some artwork that belongs to my father, Ernst Steichenhahl. By the way, that's a lovely green scarf you are wearing... Hermes, yes?"

"No, Walmart! Wrong number!" I ended the connection. By that time Karrie had hung up on me. I called her back. She answered.

"You know, my dear, I was going for a hot pink background, and then Lynny here was in the process of airbrushing some fluffy feathers in white and opalescent pink. I was going for a pink Flamingo Floridian look. Now thanks to you, the feathers look like the stripes on a barber shop pole. This was not the look I was going for."

"Karrie, stop it for a minute. Things just got worse."

"And how much worse would that be? Oh no. Not another dead vendor at the flea market? Fish didn't kick the bucket, did he?"

"No!"

"That's too bad."

"Karrie! Remember that name David gave us? Ernst Steichenhahl?"

"Oh yes, the Nazi."

"His son just called me and wants to talk about getting back his father's art. He didn't use the name Steichenhahl. He used the name Strickland."

"Oh my God. You, you have to call the police. There's no time to waste."

"I guess we know who killed Freddie. And who's been taking potshots at me."

"You can't stay alone in that wretched apartment. Pack your things and come stay with me until all this blows over. We'll figure out something about getting you a new lawyer. I have a few people who owe me some favors. This may be the right time to call one in."

I sighed. "Thank you. Listen, I probably ruined your nails. I'll let you go."

"See you tonight." Karrie hung up. I went back to the law firm and tried to throw myself into my work. The minute I had a break, I got on the phone and called David and Iceman. They agreed to meet me at Karrie's house that night.

CHAPTER 16

Iceman and David met me at Karrie's house for dinner. Somewhere between candy cane fingernails and frantic phone calls from me, Karrie cooked a pot roast drowned in a rich dark gravy, buttery whipped potatoes, and green beans almondine. She even baked a cherry pie and put on a large pot of coffee. It was going to be a long night.

Baines, David, Karrie, and I sat around the table. We were just about to start pouring coffee when there was a knock at the door. I tried to ignore that both men had their hands on their gun belts, following behind Karrie as she went to answer the door. Ever the coward, I wondered if I should be hiding under the table to avoid flying bullets.

I heard everyone talking. Karrie led the gentleman at the door into the dining room and offered him a piece of pie and a cup of coffee. I recognized him immediately. It was the lawyer from the Monmouth County prosecutor's office, Mr. Wink. Another lawyer. Great. Just who I wanted to see.

"Ms. Sanchez, I don't know if you remember me."

"I remember you. You were from the prosecutor's office. You were at that first meeting."

"Yes, at your law firm. Ms. Sanchez, let me get right to the point. You are in a lot of danger here."

"No, you think? I have a Nazi chasing me. He's a little bit peeved because he thinks I have all his artwork."

At that point, David interrupted. "No. You have the artwork stolen from victims, victims of war crimes. It is not, nor will it ever be, *his* artwork. It belongs to the families he stole from, or it belongs to the world and should be in a museum."

"What I'm going to suggest," stated Mr. Wink, "is that you meet with Steichenhahl and draw him out."

"Let me see if I've got this straight. You want to use me as bait? That never quite seems to work out for the fish." I looked over at Iceman, who stood firmly planted against the wall with his arms folded. He didn't say a word, but I got the distinct feeling that he didn't approve of any of this. But he wasn't saying anything.

"Yes, Ms. Sanchez. I would like you to try to draw him out."

"But I don't think that he'll be calling me back. I told him he had the wrong number and hung up on him. By the way, his name wasn't Steichenhahl. It was Strickland, Albrecht Strickland."

"I am sure that Mr. Steichenhahl, a.k.a. Strickland, will call you back. By the way, you know who Albrecht Strickland is?" asked David.

"No, but I think you should tell me because I really don't need any more surprises. Today was just full of them."

"Did you ever hear of Strickland Lights?"

"There isn't anyone in New Jersey who hasn't heard of them. They have half the electrical contracts all over the state."

David explained. "The Steichenhahls have owned the company for decades. Of course, the name has changed over the years, and the family moved from country to country hiding from people like me. Here is the deal that I have made with these two men here." He pointed to Iceman and Mr. Wink. "I get the art and a chance at Steichenhahl after he has been indicted for the murder of Mr. Grant. He will face more justice elsewhere. You, Ms. Roxie, have managed to do what many people my organization have not been able to do for years, and that is to draw the creep out."

"You're forgetting one important thing. I don't have the art anymore. You people took it. If I go to meet with him, I have nothing to offer this psychopath other than a not-so-friendly 'hello'. What am I supposed to say to this guy?" I slumped in my chair. "This is a nightmare. This is an absolute nightmare. I can't do this. I'm not a cop or a spy."

I looked over at Karrie and noticed that she looked thoughtful. "Why not send in a female agent or detective and say that she is Roxie?"

David sighed. "Won't work. Listen to what she said before. He commented on the color of her scarf. He was watching her, and he has her cell phone number. He knows who she is. These are very wealthy people who hire private security. Roxie, he will call you again. Make arrangements to meet him. We'll give you a painting to whet his appetite." David's eyes softened. "I understand if you don't want to do this. But I just want to assure you that if you decide to meet with these people, you will have plenty of backup."

I looked around the room at all the faces. I tried to feel out what each of them may have been thinking. Karrie looked nervous. David looked at me with pleading puppy dog eyes, but I think he would've been okay about the situation if I decided to back out. The one who was a complete puzzle was Baines. He kept very quiet and carefully watched everyone, especially me. A lot was at stake here, people lost their lives and their fortunes over this artwork. Who was I to try not to help right the wrongs of the past?

"I'm in. What do I have to do and how do you want me to do it?"

David walked over. I felt two large, strong hands on my shoulders as he bent down to whisper in my ear. I heard what he said and smiled back at him. David's cell phone rang. He began speaking in Hebrew, and the conversation seemed very serious, so he left the room. Karrie excused herself to get my bed ready upstairs with brand new sheets and blankets. This left Baines alone in the room with me...somewhat uncomfortably.

He walked over and pulled up a kitchen chair. "What did lover boy say to you?"

"Excuse me? Lover boy? Have you lost your mind?"

Baines looked at me with steady yet sensitive eyes. "Look, you don't have to do this. It's dangerous. While you'll be surrounded by state police and probably the FBI and other foreign agents, you're walking out there alone. Nobody can make this choice but you."

"Look, I need to address the lover boy thing here. There's nothing between us. He bought me dinner. And now he wants me to become his bait in a Nazi fishing expedition. First point of fact is, he is not my lover. Second point, I am not a fish. Third point, I want to know why you care so much about what David said. We're not in a relationship."

"Oh, I don't know," he sighed. "I guess I just don't want to see Calamity Jane get a bullet in her nice butt."

"What are you so worried about my derrière for?"

"You have a nice one. I just don't want to see it get splattered all over the place."

"Baines, you're killing me here."

"C'mon, Hon. What did lover boy whisper in your ear?"

"All he said was 'thank you.'"

I watched a smile come across Baines' face. It was different from the smiles I was used to that always had just a touch of sarcasm to them. He was a good-looking man who always had that look on his face with women. He was the cat and they were the canary that was going to be swallowed whole. But tonight the look in his eyes was much softer. He actually seemed to be concerned.

I guess not to be outdone by lover boy, he put his hands on my shoulders, kissed me on the top of my forehead and said, "See you tomorrow at the prosecutor's office. When he calls back, we're going to wire you up." He left the room.

Hardly the romantic line I had in mind. But given the circumstances, I'll take it.

****

I helped Karrie clean up the dinner dishes. When everything was finally washed and put away, I said good night, changed into my PJs, and headed up to my room, a large comfortable room with a big soft bed, a cushy down comforter, and marvelous fluffy pillows.

Sleep. Rest. Relax. I repeated those words over and over in my head. *Sleep. Rest. Relax.*

Finally I felt my body start relaxing, and all the panic I had felt previously was beginning to dissipate. I listened to the sound of my own breath, and I actually found I was able to calm my mind down. Then my cell phone went off. I immediately had an adrenaline rush and answered the phone.

"Hello?"

"'Hallo? Ms. Sanchez, you ran away so quickly today. And I thought we might have a chat."

"With whom am I speaking?" I asked politely. "Is this the same gentleman that asked about my scarf?"

"Yes, yes it is. Albrecht Strickland here. But my friends all call me Ulf."

"It's a little bit late for a social call, isn't it, Mr. Strickland?"

"But I insist," he answered. "You simply must call me Ulf. After all, you and I going to become good friends pretty soon."

"And how do you see us becoming friends?"

"I mean you no harm. My father would like his artwork back and you are going to give it to me. It's a simple equation, really."

"Really? How did you find me...Ulf? I'm not exactly in the Yellow Pages."

"I have my mysterious ways," he laughed. "Actually I have a friend who knows you quite well. You weren't that hard to find."

With that last line I noticed the tone in his voice darken.

"I see. When do you want to meet up so I can start unloading this artwork you're so worried about? I can't possibly do this during the day."

"Of course you can't. And neither can I. We will meet at night, at the storage place where my father left all his artwork."

I knew I was going out on a limb with the next question. "Your father has quite good taste. Where did he get the art?"

I heard what almost sounded like a low growl. "I believe that is none of your business. The only business you've got is to return the artwork to me and Father."

I felt a sudden wave of indignation come over me. "And what happens, Ulf, if I decide not to give the artwork back or maybe give the artwork to a charity? What will your father do then?"

"The prospects of that occurring are too, too horrible to think about."

"For whom?"

"For you! I will expect you at the U-STORIT facility tomorrow promptly at seven-thirty p.m. Be on time and don't bring anyone with you. Bring the key to the storage unit and that's it." He hung up the phone.

My heart was pounding and I felt blood pulsating in my ears. I was absolutely terrified. I ripped off the covers and ran downstairs. I was lucky. Karrie was still up and reading today's newspaper. When she heard my flight down the stairs she looked up.

"What's wrong?"

"Oh my God, Karrie! He called me! Strickland called me. He told me to meet him seven-thirty tomorrow night at the storage unit, and he also told me not to bring anyone. I think he's gonna kill me."

"Oh my dear. This is terrible. Call David or William. They need to know about this right now."

"Oh Karrie," I sobbed, "you had to hear his voice. He sounded so evil, so cold. I bet icicles flow through his veins."

Karrie shook her head as she looked at the clock in her living room. "Let's call the guys. They need to hear this."

****

The next morning I called in sick to work and met Baines down at the prosecutor's office later that afternoon. I was going to do this. I was going to let myself get wired so that they could catch this creep and his father. In my mind I knew there were certain risks, but this was something I felt I had to do. It felt right. I would just have to be very careful.

I had put on a camisole and Baines handed me the microphone and some tape. He was watching me until I told him that I really needed to do the rest all by myself. He asked me if I needed some help. I told him no. I taped on the small wireless mic and moved it around in my bra until I felt it was hidden from sight.

"I'm telling you again, Sanchez," he said gently, "you don't have to do this."

"And who are you going to send in? Karrie?"

He started to laugh. "While I think Ms. Karrie has some young ideas, I think she may be a little bit old for the job." He stepped back for a minute, looking thoughtful. It wasn't his usual leering "I'd love to get in your pants" look. It was one of sympathy and even caring. "I just want you to know that you won't be totally alone out there."

"How so?"

"Let's just say you'll be under a lot of watchful eyes. What time are you supposed to be meeting the U-boat commander?"

"Oh. You mean Albrecht?"

"Uh-huh."

"Seven-thirty p.m. He wants me to open the storage unit." I looked up at him. "We've got a problem, Baines. I don't have the key, and I thought you guys moved all the artwork. And confiscated it."

"We put enough back in place to make a difference. You'll see."

I had this nasty feeling in the pit of my stomach. My fear was that this was not going to end well…for me.

CHAPTER 17

The moon was a full white orb set upon the background of a midnight blue sky. A remarkable sphere, a piece of white velvet cut out in a perfect circle and pasted on top of a starless evening sky. Under any other circumstance, it would have been a romantic moon, a sensual moon, but this night it had a different meaning. For me it was a moon of vampires and werewolves that promised to bring every bit of lunacy hanging around in the ethers. This was the moon that followed me tonight.

I pulled into the parking lot of U-STORIT. The place was deserted except for the man behind the counter. I looked around, half expecting Steichenhahl, Strickland, whatever the hell his name was, to be positioned on a roof with a high-powered rifle. But if he shot me, his access to the millions of dollars' worth of artwork would be gone…at least temporarily.

I turned off my engine and rested my head on the steering wheel for a minute. I wanted to run and hide, but there was nowhere to go. I just wanted this whole thing to be over. As I sat in the parking lot, I heard the sound of tires on gravel. I had company. It was a brand new limousine, and it pulled up right next to me. The window rolled down. I rolled mine down cautiously. A man glared at me.

The guy looked like he was in his mid to late fifties. He had a refined chiseled face, a deep unnatural tan, and frightening blue eyes. A bang of streaked blond hair fell across his forehead, and both his head and his hands rested on top of an ornate walking stick. It wasn't Ernst Steichenhahl because if it was, he had somehow managed to cheat the age fairy. We stared at each other. He was the first to blink.

"Good evening, Ms. Sanchez. I am very happy to see you."

I sniffed. "Wish I could say the same, but I'd be lying."

"It is a bit chilly out tonight. Why do you not come and sit in my car for minute."

My guts were telling me this was a bad idea. "If you don't mind, I can just drive you down to where the unit is and you can take a look around."

I guess my answer was unacceptable. He pulled out a gun, pointed it at me, then gestured me inside of the back of the limousine. "I think you better come in and have a seat where it's warm."

"Are you going to shoot me?"

"Not if you do what I ask."

I had been given a special phrase to say when I thought things were getting beyond what I could handle. Right now, things were way beyond what I could handle. Except I had a problem. I'd forgotten the phrase. All I knew was that it had something to do with the night. I tried to remember: was it, "Oh, what a remarkable night?" "Tonight's the night?" "It happened one night?"

Supposedly every law enforcement agent in the world was listening to this conversation. But I didn't see any cavalry coming, and now some crazy guy was waving a gun in my face, asking me to come sit with him in the back of his limo. I kept trying to remember the phrase. I was so nervous I could barely remember my name. Of course, Strickland took the time to remind me again.

"Oh, Miss Sanchez. I'm waiting." This icy tone of the psychopath's voice went through me. Slowly I got out of the car and decided that I better do with this creep tells me.

I walked over to the limousine. The door opened and I ducked my head to get in. There are so many times in my life that I would've loved to have sat in a limousine headed to Atlantic City with a bunch of my girlfriends for on a wild night of boozing and men. But instead I was stuck in the back seat of a limo with a man pointing a gun at me. I wasn't alone in the limo, either. I turned to look at the others.

"Hail, hail. Looks like the gang's all here." Seated next to Strickland/Steichenhahl was my boss, Mr. Blackwood. Now *that* was a surprise. Next to him was Pynchard, not a surprise. Next to them were goons wearing shoulder holsters. This was it. I wasn't getting out of here alive. But dammit, I was going out with a few choice words.

"Pynchard, I expected to see you here. But Mr. Blackwood, I am really surprised at you. I thought you were too busy chasing the latest skirt in our office that you hired. You know, the one with the big boobs?"

The old guy shook his head. "You know, my dear, I tried to give you an out because I liked you. I tried to persuade you to walk away from the estate so tonight could be avoided. But you wouldn't listen. Even after I fired some warning shots in your direction. Your friend Freddie wouldn't listen either. He's no longer with us, and soon you will be joining him. You are so stubborn. Is that a Spanish girl thing?"

I noticed that Pynchard was watching but not saying a word, although he had a menacing grin across his face.

"No, Mr. Blackwood. It's not a Spanish girl thing. I really think it's a not wanting to let rich people push you around kind of thing. I'm just surprised you're involved with Umlaut over here." I noticed that Strickland got pretty angry at the sarcasm.

"I don't have any more time to waste with you, Ms. Sanchez. Just give me back my art."

"I can't give you back anything until I have the key to the storage unit. I have to get that at the front desk."

"Tell my driver where he has to go."

I nodded. I told him that he would have to go past the gates and to the first office on the left. I would get out and get the key. Strickland decided that he would come with me.

I walked into the office of U-STORIT and went to the desk. Nick Pontocurso wasn't sitting there reading a newspaper this time. Instead, there was a young man with long dark hair in a ponytail. He wore khakis. A muscular arm with a sleeve of tattoos stuck out from under the Ralph Lauren knockoff polo. He was reviewing conversations on his cell phone before he looked up.

"Can I help you?" he asked politely.

"Yeah, I'd like to have the key to my storage unit."

"And your unit number, please?"

"G-75."

"Some ID please?" I pulled out my driver's license. He looked at it quickly, then went to the back of the office to retrieve the key. As he handed me the key, he asked me if I knew where the unit was. I told him that I knew where it was because I had been there before.

I went outside and got back in the limousine with my captors. The whole situation reminded me of the title of a novel I had read about that timeless rock group, The Doors. It was called *No One Here Gets Out Alive*. Only now I was writing a book with a slightly different title: *I Don't Get out of Here Alive*. We drove to the back of a series of warehouse buildings until we finally hit G-75.

I got out and opened the lock on the large garage door, praying that they had put enough of the famous artwork back in place to make it look convincing. Strickland had also gotten out of the car with his gun still out, continuing to wave it about. Pynchard and Blackwood followed behind him. I noticed the two bodyguards had opened their holsters. Three men with guns to take me out? I mean, realistically one would've been enough. Who did they think they were killing? Wonder Woman?

I couldn't believe my eyes! Baines and company somehow managed to put everything back that they had removed. It was all covered by canvas tarps. We really couldn't see anything except maybe the edges of the picture frames that stuck out. Strickland looked excited. I watched as he turned to one of his goons.

"Franz, where is the list that Father gave you?"

I watched as Franz pulled out a yellowed, deteriorating envelope. He removed a crumpled paper from the envelope.

"Read me the name of the first painting on that list," Strickland ordered. I watched as he turned to look at me. "Let us hope, Ms. Sanchez, that everything is in place the way my father and Mr. Blackwood left it."

"You know, this place wasn't here until about ten years ago. Where did you guys stash all this stuff?"

"My garage. But I was concerned that people were going to start asking too many questions. So when the artwork left Europe and landed in my house, I held on to it until this place was built," answered Mr. Blackwood. "I have a partnership interest in this place with my friend Edward here. My other partner, Albrecht, paid me a very handsome price to help them out." He turned to his accomplice. "I am sure that you will find everything in order, Albrecht."

Strickland smiled. "I expect nothing less."

I kept trying to remember that line that I was supposed to say when things got too hot. It was awful. I could remember the town that I used to live in when I was five years old, but I couldn't remember that catchphrase I was supposed use when I was in trouble. If they were listening, which they were supposed to be, they better get their tails in here soon. I was running out of polite conversation, and I was sure they just wanted me dead.

"Enough with the idle prattle. Miss Sanchez, I want to show you some of the world's finest art now in my private collection."

I kept thinking that if my new friend, Avi Antares, was out there, no way this man was ever going to keep this art, even if I died tonight. This art had all been catalogued, and now there were records of it. Strickland was never keeping any of it.

With Franz following him, Strickland walked over to the first tarp. "What is the first painting on the list, Franz?"

"The *Portrait of Dr. Gachet* by van Gogh, Herr Strickland."

"Excellent. Miss Sanchez, you do know the history behind this painting, yes?"

"No. Not interested. You have what you want. Why not let me go?"

He ignored the question. "Dr. Gachet was the physician who treated van Gogh at an artist commune weeks before he shot himself in the chest." Strickland chuckled and shook his head.

"What's so funny about van Gogh committing suicide?"

He sniffed. "Well, it appears that van Gogh thought that Dr. Gachet was more depressed than he was. Van Gogh expressed an interpretation of Dr. Gachet in two portraits. I am about to show you one thought to be lost. A psychiatrist more depressed than the patient. Ironic, is it not? Just like you receiving an art history lesson before you are executed."

I rolled my eyes. "Just shoot me and get it over with. You're unbearable. How would you say it in fancy terms? You are a prime example of, oh, what's the word I'm looking for? Ennui."

His face grew red with anger. "Let us look together at Dr. Gachet, shall we? Sold for $82 million in 1990, and now in my rightful possession. These are the things power and money can buy." With a wave of his hand, he removed the tarp.

Underneath the tarp was an oil painting of a green-haired clown with a big red nose, wearing a hot pink polka dot clown suit. Apparently happy in his work, he juggled squirrels while seated upon a unicycle.

"Ah, Albrecht. Wow. You really hit the jackpot here. A period piece. Early 1960s kindergarten." I gave myself a closer view of the canvas. "That's Dr. Gachet? No wonder van Gogh thought he was nuts. What's with the squirrels?"

I watched as Strickland's tanned face went from red to white. He rushed over and yanked off another canvas tarp. Hidden beneath was a real treasure, Botticelli's *Birth of Venus*. But Venus had taken on an entirely different look. This Venus was a fat woman with long bleached hair, freckles, pendulous sagging breasts, and buckteeth. It was *Mad Magazine's* Alfred E. Neuman as Botticelli's Venus. A lit cigarette dangled from pouty, collagen enhanced lips. Instead of standing on a scallop shell, she balanced precariously on a rubber life raft that appeared to be deflating. Above her head floated lawn gnomes with horrified expressions, carrying a small camouflage-colored bivouac tent to drape their around the Rubenesque goddess.

At least if I was going to die, I'd die laughing. I suppressed a smile.

Panic stricken, the crazed art collector stripped off another tarp. Hiding beneath it was an army of plastic statues, small open-armed little professors, each holding a sign that said, "I Love You This Much," surrounded by rubber snakes, the kind you win at county fairs in a ring toss.

This was his prized collection of fine art? I sold better stuff at Columbia Meadows.

Before I could even laugh, Blackwood grabbed me around the throat. "You useless little witch! What did you do with my artwork? What have you done?" I couldn't talk. He was cutting off my airway. One hand let go to recoil and slap me and knock me to the ground. I gagged.

Suddenly there was a rush of air. I lay on the floor trying to catch my breath, but I forced myself to stand up. I looked at Blackwood.

"You murderous old bastard!" With that I kicked him between the legs. He moaned and dropped. I enjoyed watching him clutch himself, until something hit me on the back of the head. I grew dizzy. I remember hearing the sound of gunshots and several thuds as bodies dropped. The last thing I recall seeing was two men in a black ski masks. One of the men, whose ponytail stuck out from under the mask, had Strickland pinned to the pavement while the other man punched him in the face repeatedly and screamed, "Where's your father! Tell me!" That was my last vision before I passed out.

****

When I woke up, I was on a hospital gurney. Karrie and Iceman stood over me. I noticed that he held a bunch of flowers.

"It's me, dear. Do you recognize me?"

I was groggy and felt like I had a hangover without the booze. "Yeah, Karrie. What happened?"

Baines leaned over the gurney and put his handsome face close to mine. "You, little girl, are one tough cookie." He dropped the flowers along my bedside. "Nice kick to Blackwood's groin. We were watching, and we all sort of enjoyed that."

"What do you mean us? Who was watching? Where's David?"

"You ask a lot of questions."

"I think I'm entitled to some answers, don't you? After all I've been through?"

He got that sexy, enticing smile. "How did you like the artwork?"

"The clown was a nice touch. Where's Strickland? Is he dead?"

He gently stroked the top of my head. "No, he's not dead. Pretty beat up, but not dead. Sorry to disappoint."

"Where is he?"

"Let's just say, he's no longer in this country."

"David has him."

"Yes. And that's all I'm gonna say to you. We arrested Blackwood and Pynchard. Have them up on kidnapping, attempted murder, art theft. Don't think those two idiots will be practicing law anytime soon unless it's from behind prison bars. Listen, Sanchez, you took a pretty good knock on the head from Pynchard, and you need to rest. When you're feeling better, I'll give you more of the details."

Karrie piped up. "My dear, when they discharge you, I want you to stay with me until you are healed up. After all, you've been busy catching murderers." She giggled. "And now you have to rest."

Baines smiled at Roxie. "If I were you, I would do what she asks. And by the way, I hear that she's a fantastic cook."

"Yeah, that's half my problem. I'm going to get fat living with her for any length of time."

Karrie's eyes twinkled. "Detective Baines, I have a wonderful idea. Providing our little girl here gets released from the hospital in a day or so, let's have a celebration at my house. I'll roast a turkey with my famous cranberry chestnut stuffing, potatoes, candied sweet potatoes with chunks of pineapple, and a delicious pumpkin pie."

His eyes lit up. "You just hit on all my favorite foods at once," he laughed. "What time is dinner?"

"The fashionable dinner time, of course. Eight o'clock sharp, and dress is casual but neat. Listen, I want to get myself a cup of coffee. Why don't you two chat?" With that last line, Karrie giggled, then hurried away pretending that she had something important to do. She wanted to leave us alone.

It was awkward. Baines hovered over me like a gentle giant. I pulled myself up a little bit, trying to resist the urge to throw my arms around his broad shoulders. "I guess I owe you my thanks. I mean, I really thought I was gonna die in that room yesterday. And the last thing my eyes would see would have been a green-haired clown on a unicycle and a fat Venus."

He gently stroked her head. "You were very brave to do what you did. You inadvertently stumbled upon an art ring run by a bunch of killers."

"What about Freddie? Did anyone confess to killing him? Had to be one of those guys. I bet it was Blackwood."

"Yeah. It's a toss-up. I think Blackwood's the man, with Pynchard as a close second." He stroked my hair. "You need to rest. I'm going to take Karrie home."

He kissed my forehead. I felt an electric shock go from the top of my forehead through my chest, into my stomach and down my legs all the way down to my toes. It was frightening. *If this is what one kiss on the forehead can do, what will happen to me when he...*

Oh my God... too overwhelming to think about.

CHAPTER 18

Three days later, I came home from the hospital. I took Karrie up on her offer to stay with her until I was fully recovered. I felt much better, but I decided that playing "Couch Commando" on Karrie's overstuffed family room sofa for a few days wasn't a terrible idea. There was a steady stream of food, coffee, ice cream, and good conversation. It was a far cry from my apartment. At Karrie's house I was warm, cozy, well fed, and comforted by my best friend.

After taking a nap before dinner, I took a long, comfortable shower. Before I even knew it, eight o'clock had arrived. The house smelled of a Thanksgiving feast. I looked in the kitchen and saw Karrie remove a succulent turkey from the oven. She scooped out the stuffing from inside and put it in a large bowl.

"Karrie, is there anything I can do to help? I feel guilty. I've been lying around like a big lump and you've been feeding me."

"Nonsense. You just got the crap beaten out of you, and you were nearly killed. The doctor told me that you needed to rest, and you shall. But if you want to help me, you can start putting the salads and the potatoes on the table so that when that handsome detective gets here, I don't have to get up and down."

"Sounds like a plan." I grabbed a few different serving bowls, most of which were exquisite Depression glass, and placed everything on her mahogany dining room table. I noticed that she had removed a leaf to make the table into a cozy square rather than a long rectangle. She had set the table with beautiful linen napkins in crystal napkin rings and her best Tiffany sterling silver place settings. Karrie was very elegant and classy. How I wished I could be like her! Even the simplest things Karrie did were accomplished with such panache.

When everything was set up on the table, she and I sat down and waited.

Eight o'clock. Eight-fifteen. Eight-thirty. No sign of Baines. My heart sank.

I looked at Karrie. "He's not here yet. I guess he's not coming. How could I have been so stupid?"

"Roxie, what you talking about?"

"You know, for a minute I really thought he cared about me, just a little bit. What was I thinking? He needed to use me as bait, that's why he was nice to me."

"Nonsense, Roxie. I saw the way he looked at you. There's more there than you think."

"I wish I could believe you." Tears started to sting my eyes. "But I don't."

"Now, now something probably happened down at the station house. Remember, he is a police officer. Things happen. I think that we should start eating. Do me a favor. Go into the second drawer near the kitchen sink and get the carving set that's in there. By the time I'm finished carving this buzzard, I think your boyfriend will be here. Cheer up." She winked. "We have a lovely meal here and a fully stomach heals all."

"I give it a try. What am I looking for?"

"First carving knife you can scare up. Look in the draw to the left."

I went to the kitchen and over to the drawer she indicated. I found everything but the carving set. The drawer was a mess. It was unlike Karrie to have a disorganized drawer. I started removing things and placing them on the counter as I looked for the set. I found one piece of it.

My heart sank. I whispered, "Oh no, please, please don't let this be true."

I remembered the day that Detective Baines showed me the carved cherry Bakelite knife that was found in Freddie's chest. Deep at the bottom of Karrie's drawer was the carved cherry Bakelite fork – it was the other half of the murder weapon. And I had just found it in my best friend's kitchen. I didn't know what to do. Karrie walked into the kitchen.

"Did you find the carving set?" she asked.

"No, no, I'm still searching around for it. What color is it?"

"Oh my dear, it's easy to recognize. It's cherry Bakelite."

"Yeah," I said, "just like the handle on the knife that was sticking out of Freddie when I found him in the van." I stood in the door way with the fork.

I watched as the face of the woman I thought was my angel twisted into the face of an angry sociopath. "How dare you!"

"How dare I what, Karrie?" I sighed. "Blackwood didn't kill Freddie. You did."

Karrie folded her arms. She wasn't remorseful, or upset. She was indignant, arrogant and angry. "What do they say these days? You shouldn't have gone there? Let me tell you something–I'm glad he's dead. And I would do it again. He destroyed my Apache burden basket. It was made with paints from plants and berries that no longer exist, a rarity from the middle of the nineteenth century. Blake and Faraday's was interested in buying it for $18,000. And what did he do? In a drunken state he falls into my table and destroys my beautiful basket. And now I have nothing."

"Was that any reason to take a man's life? For a basket?"

"Of course, it was! That basket was in our family for years. It was my great grandmothers given to her by an Apache woman who worked for her. Those baskets symbolize guardianship of the home, and were used in Apache Nation rituals. He destroyed something magnificent and beautiful. He destroyed history. Just like you're doing right now. You've destroyed a wonderful friendship that would've lasted the rest of your life. You were the daughter I never had! And now you betrayed me!"

Her eyes grew wild, her breathing was rapid. She became crazier by the second. I had to somehow get out of there and get to the police.

"Karrie, I think I should go now."

"Oh no, no, no, my dear. You are not going anywhere." She reached into another kitchen drawer and pulled out her derringer.

"You know, I never refinished the cellar, never had time to lay the concrete. That'll be your final resting place. Your police officer boy-friend isn't coming anyway. I called him and canceled dinner. After all, you still aren't feeling well, and I can't have him snooping around here."

"Karrie, why are you doing this? Look, there are all kinds of defenses to murder. Heat of passion – this could change from murder to involuntary manslaughter."

"Yes, but in order to downgrade, as they say, I would have to have lacked intent or committed the crime with reckless disregard for the safety and welfare of others. Isn't that the standard? You work for lawyers you should know. I wasn't going to pay anyone to kill him. It was cheaper to do it myself."

"Good grief what are you talking about?"

"Call it murder at a market rate. But this is even better, it was a flea market rate, Yes! Yes! The cheap, effective killing of a nobody. I plotted it for months after he destroyed my beautiful basket. That rare piece of Native American art survived for a hundred years, and he destroyed it in a matter of seconds in one of his vodka-fueled stupors. I'm just *sorry* that I wasted a very expensive set of Bakelite utensils on that buffoon." I noticed that she kept her hand steady on the Derringer which was pointed directly at my heart.

I closed my eyes and prayed it would be quick.

"Goodbye, Roxie. You are one of the best friends I ever had. I will really miss you…"

"Mrs. Langston, I am disappointed in you. Drop the gun and put your hands in the air."

It was Baines. He had his nine millimeter Glock pointed right at her head. I couldn't believe it. I was never so happy to see this gorgeous hunk of man in my entire life. "Sanchez, you still have the other half of that murder weapon set?"

"The fork that goes with the knife?"

"I said drop the weapon Karrie! Do it!"

Karrie let the gun fall to the floor, as she muttered something beneath her breath.

"Yeah. The knife that killed Freddie was a rare cherry Bakelite 1940s Sheffield staghorn carving set. It was patterned after deer antlers, the made in cherry red Bakelite. We looked at all the local antique stores, and it turns out that our good friend Karrie here purchased the set on eBay for fifty dollars two weeks before she killed Freddie. No matter how much we sweated them and their lawyers. Blackwood and Pynchard denied killing him"

"Oh, Karrie, you were my friend. I feel very sorry for you."

She turned her head. "I really don't care how you feel."

Tears poured down my face as I heard other police vehicles arrive. Karrie put her head down, more or less admitting defeat. I watched as a bunch of uniformed officers shuffled in, cuffed her and took her away.

It was more than I could take. I rushed over to Baines and fell into his arms. It was the one place I wanted to be. He drew me close to him and we kissed.

"It's okay Sanchez," he stated. "I will always be here for you."

****

The alarm clock rang, and it was Sunday again. I hopped into the shower at four a.m. Baines had helped me load the truck the night before, so I was ready to go. In the recent days that had passed, I received phone calls from the Columbia Meadows crew: Bug Eye Betty, Fish, JJ, Red Hawk, and Lottie. The whole flea market was buzzing about Karrie's arrest and the murder charge. Some people were relieved; others, well, not so much. It was kind of uncomfortable for the simple folk at Columbia Meadows to know that there was a murderer in their midst and no one knew about it. Out of all the Columbia Meadows club members, Fishy McClure was the most devastated about Karrie's arrest. He referred to Karrie as his "last love." Everyone knew his first love was cheap beer.

I was just relieved to know that nobody was going to be out there trying to kill me. Blackwood and Pynchard were in jail. Freddie's sisters had curiously dropped their lawsuit against me and agreed to cooperate with the Monmouth County Prosecutor against the two men. The artwork, for the most part, went back to either the museums that first housed the pieces or the descendants of the owners, if the original owners were no longer alive. Each piece of art found in the U-STORIT unit had finally found a home. This brought me a new comfort along with my newfound lover, Detective William Baines.

As I was setting up, my cell phone went off. It was Baines. "I thought you would be getting your beauty sleep at this time of the morning," I said, only half-joking.

"I was. Look at your cell phone."

"Yeah?" I looked at the smartphone in my hand. It wasn't mine. I had grabbed Baines' phone by mistake. "Aw, hon, I have your phone. I hope no strange women will be calling you on it. Sorry."

"You're going to be even sorrier when I tell you who called you on your cell phone."

"And who might that be? I'm afraid to ask."

"Some guy with a strange accent looking for something he called Picasso's sketchbook. Know anything about it, Sanchez? What the hell were you and Karrie doing? You girls are killing me."

I took a deep breath. "I have to call you back. Customers are coming."

An elegantly dressed elderly man came up to my table. "My goodness, you have such lovely old things. Old things, like me."

"Thank you." I was always good with accents. His was a distinct German accent, but with a very soft inflection.

He picked up an old Swiss music box. With large gentle fingers he wound up the old music box. It tinkled a version of Strauss's Blue Danube Waltz. His accent was distinctly German, and his clothes looked expensive, tailored and pressed. He closed his eyes became absorbed by the music as he spoke in a soft, dulcet tone.

"A lovely old piece. I had one like this when I was a child. It works properly, yes?"

"Sure does." I looked at the man's face. Hmmm, it looked strangely familiar. The clothing he wore was way too expensive. He had a scarf and draped it around his neck in a manner that had a

European flair to it. He appeared too wealthy for a someone perusing a flea market.

"May I ask how much for this music box?"

"Thirty dollars." I looked at the man's face. It was an older man's face, but still quite handsome with a strong jaw.

"I'll take it, my dear Do you have a box? Ah, you must forgive me. I am old, and I must ask for my assistants to help me carry my purchases." The dapper old gentlemen nodded his head in the direction of two younger men dressed in suits. They immediately came over stood alongside of the old man. They didn't talk; they didn't smile. Both men stood their and glared at me.

"Give me a moment, Sir, I think I can find one." I walked to back of my SUV, and started digging around for a box that was large enough to hold the music box.

"Fraulein, I also have another question. I was wondering if you had any artwork for sale."

I felt my heart race. When I heard the word "Fraulein" and the request for artwork, a lump rose in my throat. I took a deep breath before turning around.

"I have several pieces of art and statuary. What exactly are you looking for, sir?"

"Oh, something I have lost called Picasso's sketch book. Have you seen it?"

How would he know about Picasso's sketch book. I thought. *That was stolen years ago.*

I could feel my blood pressure rising. Now I knew who he was.

"You know Fraulein, my son is in jail now because of what you did. Naughty girl. What other treasures have you stolen from me, eh?"

"Mr. Strickland given what I have learned, I think you're the *real* thief."

"Use your words carefully, Fraulein. The past has a way of coming back to haunt you."

At which point, one of the young men standing next to Strickland opened his coat and showed me a holstered gun. I felt nauseous, and light-headed. My eyes widened and my mind began to conjure up negative thoughts.

Here we go again, I thought. *Is he going to kidnap me or just shoot me in broad daylight?*

Then all of a sudden, the horrible feelings vanished as quickly as they had come. Across Aisle 67 I saw Avi Antares and a few of his little, or should I say rather large, size friends. They were staring at Strickland and his goons. I guess Avi hadn't left country after all.

I was thrilled. Avi and his troupe began to quietly creep up behind Strickland and his henchmen.

"Did you hear what I said Fraulein?"

"About the past?" I smiled. "Oh yes. The past does come back to haunt you, Strickland. Especially when you *least* expected it.